CHARTBREAK

Oh sure, you know exactly what happened in the very beginning. You know and I know and the vicarandthepostmanandthewindowcleaner and the whole WORLD know the story. You must have heard the record, even if you didn't buy it, and you probably read some of the interviews as well. And saw the video.

Well, kids, sorry to disappoint you, but you can forget all that. Because that's not quite how it was, not in real life. To begin with, I hadn't actually run away from home. Just stamped out in a temper after another family row . . .

Gillian Cross has been writing children's books for over twenty years. Before that, she took English degrees at Oxford and Sussex Universities; and she has done various jobs, including working in a village bakery, and being an assistant to a Member of Parliament. She is married with four children and lives in Warwickshire. Her hobbies include orienteering and playing the piano.

Other titles by Gillian Cross include:

Tightrope
ISBN 0 19 271750 2 (paperback)
ISBN 0 19 271804 5 (hardback)

Eddie Beale looks after his friends, people say, as long as they entertain him. When he takes notice of Ashley, she is happy to put on a show and be part of the excitement that surrounds him and his gang—it is a relief from the unrelenting drudgery of her life. Then she realizes that someone is watching her. Someone is stalking her and leaving messages that get uglier and uglier. Can Eddie help her? And if he does, what price will she have to pay?

The Great Elephant Chase
ISBN 0 19 271786 3

Winner of the Smarties Prize and the Whitbread Children's Novel Award

'An undoubted classic.'
The Sunday Times

Wolf
ISBN 0 19 271784 7

Winner of the Carnegie Medal

'An outstanding achievement.'
The Times Educational Supplement

Pictures in the Dark
ISBN 0 19 271741 3

'This is in the best tradition of Gillian Cross's novels . . . a tremendously strong emotional range and an acute awareness of the stress of growing up.'
School Librarian

Chartbreak

Other Oxford fiction:

The House of Rats
Stephen Elboz

Starlight City
Sue Welford

Outcast
Rosemary Sutcliff

Flambards
K. M. Peyton

A Pack of Lies
Geraldine McCaughrean

Chandra
Frances Mary Hendry

It's My Life
Michael Harrison

Against the Day
Michael Cronin

Chartbreak

Gillian Cross

OXFORD
UNIVERSITY PRESS

Great Clarendon Street, Oxford OX2 6DP

Oxford University Press is a department of the University of Oxford.
It furthers the University's objective of excellence in research, scholarship,
and education by publishing worldwide in

Oxford New York

Athens Auckland Bangkok Bogotá Buenos Aires Calcutta
Cape Town Chennai Dar es Salaam Delhi Florence Hong Kong Istanbul
Karachi Kuala Lumpur Madrid Melbourne Mexico City Mumbai
Nairobi Paris São Paulo Singapore Taipei Tokyo Toronto Warsaw

with associated companies in Berlin Ibadan

Oxford is a registered trade mark of Oxford University Press
in the UK and in certain other countries

First published 1986
Reprinted 1987, 1989

First published in this paperback edition 1999

British Library Cataloguing in Publication Data available

ISBN 0-19-275043 7

Typeset by Fontwise, with revisions by Mike Brain Design

Printed in Great Britain by
Cox & Wyman Ltd, Reading, Berkshire

'Save Your Breath' is quoted by kind permission
of Elizabeth Cross

PERSONAL FILE

Finch (Kelp)

Name: Janis Mary Finch

Born: Of course I was. Seventeen years ago, in Birmingham.

Nickname at school: Oh, they probably called me all sorts of things, but I wouldn't know what. Never spoke to any of them if I could help it.

Have you ever been on a diet? Look, my only problem with food is getting enough. I'm five foot eleven and it's twelve stone of bone and muscle, not flab. Want me to come round and demonstrate?

Other bands you've sung with? There isn't any band worth joining except Kelp.

Do you play any games or sports? I used to put the shot at school, but now I'm into martial arts. Karate mostly, but I'm very interested in ninjitsu and everything about the ninjas. That's why I wear a ninja suit on stage—and off as well, quite often.

Favourite drink: Water

Is 'Face It' really a true account of how you met up with the band? Yes. Job wrote the words as well as the tune, but he was drawing on things I'd told him.

Have you got any pets? Not yet. But I'm going to buy an ocelot. That's a small wild cat from South America. Fantastically fierce and beautiful.

What was the first record you bought? Don't remember.

Does Dave really play all those different instruments? Yes. *And* he cleans his own teeth and cuts his own toe-nails. He's unbelievably talented.

Whose music has influenced you most? Christie Joyce's. And if you want to know who influenced *him*, you'll have to ask him.

What have you got in your pockets? My ninja suit doesn't have pockets. Rollo always carries my money for me.

Most important concert: The concert in Nottingham on our first tour, when we supported Nitrogen Cycle. That's when everything came 100% right for the first time. An amazing feeling.

What's your bedroom like? A prison cell. Well, no, it's a bit more comfortable than that. I don't share it, for a start. But it's just a room with a wardrobe for clothes and a bed for sleeping. I'm not into interior decoration.

Have you got a boyfriend? I eat boyfriends for breakfast.

OK. What did you have for breakfast this morning? Oh, this morning I only had sausages and eggs and chips. I wasn't really hungry.

Now, can we ask you about the band's first-ever Top of the Pops appearance? Groan. I knew that would be bound to come up.

Well, everyone's always wanted to know. What was going on? Look, there's no way I can tell you in a couple of words for an interview like this. I couldn't begin to explain it properly without going way back. Right back to the very beginning, in fact.

Smash Hits

Chapter 1

Oh sure, you know exactly what happened in the very beginning. *You* know and *I* know and the vicarandthe-postmanandthewindowcleaner and the whole WORLD know the story. You must have heard the record, even if you didn't buy it, and you probably read some of the interviews as well. And saw the video.

Remember it?

That grey, grainy opening sequence with me drooping over my cup in the motorway café, suitcase at my feet and a tatty school scarf draped round my neck. Stirring my coffee with no sound except the chink of the spoon against the cup. Then my voice starts up, very high and clear and slow, with Dave's harmonica as the only backing.

> *'Came out of Birmingham with nothing*
> *Junked the name and face I used to wear*
> (a long swoop on the harmonica and then two little notes)
> *When your flesh and blood don't give a damn*
> (voice and harmonica climbing together, long-drawn-out and very faintly flat)
> *Your luggage doesn't hold much from before'*

And, as I sing, my head on the screen looks up and there's a blank where my face ought to be. But down in my coffee cup the black and white reflection of my face stares up, shifting and changing all the time. Sad, happy, tough, leering, bored . . . changing clothes and wigs and make-up. Pentathlete, lion-tamer, karate *sensei*, headmistress . . . clown, mafia boss, geisha, prime minister. . . . That bit of the video took about a week to shoot—I think we produced five different versions in the end—and I got to try all my fantasies on for size.

Then the drums take over from the harmonica as I go into the second verse. A very strong, steady beat.

'My last coins went to pay for coffee
(and Christie's voice begins on the rap, spiky and sarcastic underneath my melody)
Strange reflections by the motorway
Then the place exploded with the band
(and the sharp words of the rap soft but very clear under my long climbing notes)
And there was music in the sad café'

Three harsh descending notes from Christie, dragged out almost unbearably, until you could scream, until, suddenly,

SPLASH!

In slow motion, the reflection in the coffee shatters, the surface breaks, spraying up against the light in a shower of coloured drops and I stand up and flex my arms, bursting out of my school uniform like the Incredible Hulk bursting out of his clothes, scattering strips of navy blue and white over the table and wrenching off my tie to throw it out of the window. And sound matches vision as the music breaks and expands, with Rollo's drumbeat subtly altering rhythm. Dave moves from harmonica to guitar, Job brings in the melody of the chorus on the electric piano the three of them singing it, very hard and steady.

'Put your body where your mind is . . .'

And way above everything, over all the instruments and the tune, high and clear and fierce, my voice and Christie's singing scat at each other, like glittering scribble, beyond sense, driving each other on and on and on. . . .

Like listening to diamonds.
Even now, that video still gives me a shiver when I watch it and I'm still getting the letters it sparked off.

> *Dear Finch,*
> *I sat in a motorway café for* weeks, *but nothing like that happened to me. . . .*

> *. . . Scratchwood. 11.30 a.m. on Friday the 14th. O.K? See you there. . . .*

> *. . . I wish, I* wish *I was as brave as you. I'd throw everything into a suitcase and run off tomorrow if I thought I stood a chance of meeting Dave. . . .*

Or Rollo or Job.
Or Christie Joyce.

Well, kids, sorry to disappoint you, but you can forget all that. Because that's not quite how it was, not in real life. To begin with, I hadn't actually run away from home. Just stamped out in a temper after another family row.

You know the script as well as I do. They start on one thing and then it broadens out to take in everything that's wrong with you and your clothes and your character and your friends—until you feel like a pimple on the face of the world.

I could just about survive rows like that when it was Mum and Dad both going on at me together, because then it was O.K. to lose my temper and stamp about and punch the furniture. But after Dad took off, when it was just Mum and me, they got unbearable. I was already bigger than her by then and if I shouted down at her it felt like I was kicking her in the face. Besides, when things got really bad, I was more likely to cheer than shout if she dredged up the energy to nag at me at all.

And then Himmler came. I hated him from the second Mum told me he was moving in with us and after six months we were barely speaking. He was always *there,* with his ginger moustache and his watery blue eyes, chipping in to add his bit to any argument. The only way I could cope was by staying icy-cold. If we had a row, I'd get more and more silent, concentrating on trying to make *him* lose his temper and shout. But it wasn't easy.

That particular day, the row started because I'd skipped school. The place was driving me insane. The teachers insisted on treating us as though we were still little kids playing What Will You Be When You Grow Up. Oh zowie. You'd need to be really thick to believe in careers for people like us. But teachers think that if you say a thing often enough it gets to be true. And so every now and again I had to get out or go mad. But this time some *kind* person had told Mum.

She was the one who started the row, at tea, very white-faced and angry, slopping the stew on to my plate as she spoke.

'Why do you have to be such an *idiot,* Jan? You used to be so good at everything.' (Sure, sure. Janis Mary, champion singer, sportswoman and school mug.) 'I really hoped there was something ahead for you. And now you can't even be bothered—' Her voice wobbled and Himmler put his bony white hand over hers and squeezed it.

'Janis,' he said, softly.

I didn't waste time answering. Just looked at the ginger hairs on the backs of his fingers while I waited for the bleeding hearts bit. And along it came.

'Janis, look what you're doing to your mum. She can't bear to see you throwing the rest of your life away. If you don't do well at school, how are you going to get a job? Never heard of unemployment?'

Sure, sure I know plenty about unemployment, Himmler. It's what your generation's cooked up as a treat for mine. But I wasn't stupid enough to say it out loud. If I did, I'd be liable to lose control. Instead, I looked down, watching Mum from under my eyelashes to see if she'd have the guts to take charge of the conversation again.

But when she came in, it was backing him up. Of course.

'Why don't you listen to Graham when he's talking to you?'

Why doesn't he listen to me, Mum? I'm the one you should be supporting. I screwed up my hands, under the table, to stop myself speaking. There's no way you can pretend to be fragile and pathetic when you're twice the size of everyone else in the room.

Himmler's horrible fingers tightened and his thumb stroked the side of Mum's hand. 'It's all right, Barbie. Don't let her get to you.'

She's my mother. I'm supposed to get to her. I had to let something out, but it mustn't be that, so I attacked instead. 'Why are you always laying into *me*? Why am *I* the one who's no good? I suppose you two are super-virtuous and respectable and—'

Himmler's moustache twitched and his face began to go pink. Got him where it hurt! One more good insult and I'd have him shouting at me like a lout in the street. That would shatter his smug, patronizing act.

'Models of respectability, aren't you?' I jeered. 'Why don't you sort *yourselves* out before—'

Out of the blue, Mum smacked the side of my head. She hadn't done it in years—it would have been ridiculous—but now she lashed out hard with the flat of her hand, yelling and screaming.

'Stop it, Jan, stop it! You're getting to be a horrible girl! *Stop!*'

Oh, she didn't hurt me, of course. Not with her hand. But it knocked me off centre, her going for me like that in front of Himmler, and I whipped round and screeched back at her.

'Better than being a tart!'

There was a second of terrible silence. Just enough space for me to realize I'd gone right over the top. Then Himmler made for me and I raced for the door, to get away from both of them.

By the time I was half-way through it, I wanted to tell her I was sorry, but when I looked over my shoulder I couldn't see her. Himmler was in between us, with his arms round her, and all I could see was his back. Scrambling out of the room, I snatched up my navy-blue school mac—because it was the nearest coat—and got myself out of the front door fast, grabbing my bike on the way to the gate.

'Jan!' Mum banged on the window. 'Don't be silly. It's raining.'

It was too. A nasty steady drizzle. Rough. I wasn't going back for hours. Putting my head down, I pedalled as hard as I could into the darkness, not aiming anywhere in particular.

But then the drizzle changed to real rain, the hard, cold sort that stings your face and trickles down your hair into your eyes. I wasn't going to let it drive me home, but I had to find somewhere to shelter. Swerving into the kerb, I tipped the money out of my purse and counted it. Just enough. I wiped the rain out of my eyes and pushed off again, heading for the motorway.

That's right. The famous café. I quite often sneaked there, by way of the path that led into the back of the car-park. I liked to sit high above the road, watching the traffic streak north to Scotland and south to London. And Paris and Africa and the world. When I was really off with everything, I'd stare down at the traffic and think, *One day I'll hitch a lift with a friendly truckie and take off down the road.*

Not that day, though. By the time I got to the car-park, my hair was soaked, plastered down close to my head and straggling six inches down my back in thick, brown rats' tails. I didn't need a mirror to tell me I looked like a heavyweight boxer. Every week I spent hours blow-drying my hair to get it soft and waving and bouncy, to disguise that boxer's face. Oh well, so what? I didn't feel like talking anyway, so the worse I looked the better. I wrenched off my school tie, shoved it in my pocket and hid my bike in the bushes. Then I put my head down and dived across the car-park towards the café.

It was three-quarters empty. A couple of tables of truckies eating enormous fry-ups. A family with three whining kids. A middle-aged man in a suit who let his eyes flicker over me and then turned back to his fish and chips. I counted out my pennies and bought a cup of black coffee. (Yes. Really.) Then with exactly four pence left, I headed for my favourite seat by the window. Marge and Annie, the two ratty little women behind the counter, glared after me and muttered to each other. I knew they didn't like me hanging round there, but I ignored them and settled myself with my coffee, gazing down at the road.

It was like magic. Even then, when I was wet and miserable, the lights of the moving traffic wiped everything else out. Time switched off and there was nothing except the reflection of my face, floating huge and ghostly in front of me in the window and, through it and below, the busy, bright lights racing red and white, sixty, eighty, a hundred miles an hour. Peace. Space.

Then, suddenly, it all went smash.

There were shouts of laughter on the stairs, loud enough to make heads turn as the door banged open. Rollo, Job and Dave erupted into the café like a trio of parrots, shrieking at a joke and vibrating with colour: Rollo's long yellow tweed coat; Dave's hat with the green feathers; Job's maroon scarf. Someone had scarlet trainers and someone else was wearing a pale yellow T-shirt screen-printed with a beautiful banana in brown and deep yellow, like an exhibit from an art gallery. They looked stylish and weird, both at the same time, and everyone in the café gaped at them as they stood there, all three of them tall and fair and laughing.

But not identical. Even in that first startled look, I was taking in the differences. Dave was the original blond bombshell, a golden beach-boy with show-off muscles and a film star's tan. Rollo was quieter, glancing round to see if their noise had upset anyone. Big, gentle hands and a slow smile, like a lovely, clumsy Labrador. And Job was so fair he was almost silver, like moonlight on water. Over six foot, like the other two, but slighter and older, with fine, tense lines round his mouth.

And then Christie came through the door after them and

no one looked at the others any more.

You may be able to imagine the scene, but the characters are too familiar now for you to catch the first shock of it, there in that scabby café. The first time I saw Christie Joyce. There was nothing to explain the effect he had. Now I almost take it for granted, but then it seemed crazy. Why should a pale, skinny boy, with dark hair and black sweat-shirt and jeans snatch all the attention away from the other three who look so sensational? Christie even had spots then, but not like other boys, who shuffle about and try to hide them and wash with medicated soap. He had spots as if he had grown them on purpose to annoy the world. They were like the rest of him. Angry. Deliberate. Impossible to ignore. He stood in the doorway looking slowly round the café while the others fetched his food for him.

His eyes moved from table to table and I saw people glance away, talking too loudly as they started to eat again. He was staring them out, coldly, as rude as if he'd stood there shouting, *Mind your own business*. Something about that look made my teeth grind. After all, he and his friends were the ones who'd come crashing in, disturbing everyone else. Why shouldn't people look at them? He certainly wasn't going to make me turn my eyes meekly away. As his face swivelled towards my table, I locked my eyes into position and glared back, stare for stare. Nothing flirty or girlish about it. The same direct, rude stare that he was giving me.

I'm not sure what I expected. Certainly not a climb-down. He wasn't the sort to swallow defeat and drop his eyes. But the others were moving towards him with trays of food and he could have made that an excuse to give up. He didn't though. Still glaring just as fiercely, he jerked his head to make the others follow and began to march across to my table.

When I was small, standing near the edge of railway platforms used to make me breathless, half from fear and half from a terrible fascination, like a soft voice saying, *Jump!* It was like that in the café, with Christie coming towards me. The sensible thing to do was to let my eyes drift away over his shoulder. If I ignored him, he would get bored in the end and go away. I'd done it before in that café, more than once, to get rid of some man who was bothering me. All I had to do was look out of the window. But the crazy part of my mind was saying, *Jump!* and I kept staring.

He sat down opposite me and let Rollo hand him a plate of spaghetti. Then, as the others filled up the empty seats at the table, he spoke for the first time.

'Nobody stares me down. Nobody.'

Just telling me. A perfectly flat voice, not angry or teasing. Keeping the same steady stare, almost without a blink, he began to eat his spaghetti with a fork. It was creepy. Out of the corner of my eye, I could see his hand moving like a piece of machinery, twirling the long strands of spaghetti and lifting them to his mouth with never a loose end or a drop of sauce flicked on his chin. I can't do that even when I'm looking at the plate.

But I *wasn't* going to look away. All day, all month, all *year* I'd been knuckling under to people. Mum, Himmler, teachers—everyone. I'd let them put me down and shove me around without lashing out, and now here was a perfect stranger getting in on the act. Well this time I had nothing to lose by being aggressive and I wasn't going to be shoved. I clamped my mouth shut, tried to keep my breathing steady and went on glaring. But the effort was starting to make me sweat. The more I stared, the harder and colder the eyes staring back seemed to become.

It was Job who got me off the hook. I didn't realize, until I knew him better, that it must have been done on purpose. I thought it was just an accidental remark, quietly muttered to Dave.

'Eat up, sunshine. If we take more than ten minutes or so over this we'll be late for the gig.'

He might just as well have said, *Relax. Cut the agony. You only have to hang on until we go.* And once I had a limit, of course, it was easy. I even allowed myself a scornful snort.

'A *gig?* You're not telling me you're some kind of band?'

'Yes,' said Christie. His voice was still level. Only a quick flicker of his eyes showed that he was annoyed with Job. 'We're a band.' Slowly, deliberately, as if that was what he had intended all the time, he looked down at his plate.

'Huh!' I grinned, easy now, enjoying the upper hand. 'What are *you,* then? The organ-grinder's monkey?'

'I'm the singer.'

I should have known, from the edge in his voice, should have seen how he was leading me on. But I was full of myself, cocky at not giving in over the staring. 'You're the *singer?* That must be brilliant. Like a gerbil squeaking away in a cage full of lions.'

'Cream!' muttered Job. He always likes a good phrase. And Rollo gave a sudden delighted splutter beside me, as if he had just been told a rude joke.

'Think you could do better, do you?' Christie said. And I walked straight into it, with both feet.

'I bet I could do it better than *you*. I can sing.'

'O.K.' He clicked the fingers of his left hand. 'Go on, then.'

'What?' I blinked.

'Sing. Let's hear you. If you're so great it would be a shame to miss the chance.' He put the last forkful of spaghetti into his mouth and leaned back, folding his arms.

You sneaky little. . . . He was at least a couple of inches shorter than me and I reckoned I could push him over with one hand, but he knew he had me on a string. And I could tell from his expression that he was looking forward to hearing my excuses. He'd failed to make me back down one way, so he was trying another.

Well, he was going to fail that way, too! What did I care about the people in the café and Marge and Annie grumping away behind the counter? I didn't need to be afraid of singing. In fact, if I'd been into being a good girl and getting pats on the head, I'd have been rehearsing solos with old Meredith and his nest of singing birds at that very moment, instead of sitting on my own looking down at the motorway. It would take more than a dare like that to make me back down. Taking a deep breath, I launched into the first song that came into my head.

It was 'Down and Out'. Remember it? A bouncy, moronic song of Happy Birthday's. It was Number One that week and it chirped at you everywhere. The tune's O.K., if you like that sort of plastic rubbish, but the words are pure, distilled *puke*. So I exaggerated them, gazing into Christie's eyes and drooling the notes out in a syrupy, sentimental way, to embarrass him.

> 'Down *and out!*
> *Baby, when I found you I was*
> Down *and out!*
> *Just lying around*
> *Waiting to be found*
> Out! *and down, down down.'*

Heads began to turn then, all over the café, but I was only just starting. The words of the verse were a million times worse than the chorus and I gave them all the drool I had.

> *'Then you came by—you looked so*
> *Fantastic!*
> *My heart started doing*
> *Gymnastics!*
> *Now the spring in my step is*
> *Elastic!*
> *As I bounce up, right up in the air. . . .'*

Somewhere in the middle there, Dave pulled out his harmonica and began to play, and Job and Rollo were whistling along, very softly, enjoying the joke. But there was no reaction from Christie, not even a twitch of an eyebrow. I took a deep breath and got ready to belt out the chorus again. I was going on until he moved or spoke or something, even if it killed me.

What he actually did caught me on the hop. At the first

note of the chorus, he came in suddenly, very high, singing a sort of lunatic, wordless cats'-cradle that danced about over the tune, playing tricks with it. For the first two bars I wanted to block my ears, to shut out his voice, and then I was hooked by it. You know what it's like, that metallic, slightly nasal whine. You don't like it, but it's bang on the note and quite different from everything else, and somehow you can't stop listening to it.

As Christie began, the other three started to sing the words of the chorus, solidly, steadily and very deadpan, like an anchor to hold down Christie's musical aerobatics. And then—well, it was like a blurred picture coming suddenly sharp into focus. I got the hang of what Christie was doing and I thought, *I can do that too*. Leaving the tune, I let my voice rise to join his, not copying his swoops and twists but answering him back, taunting and teasing and egging him on to produce more and more complicated patterns. We were staring at each other again, but this time we were both hanging on, keeping our eyes in close contact while our voices stretched and spiked and racketed about. And all the time the voice inside my head was shouting, *I can do this!*

But before we could build up to doing something really good with the next verse, there were shouts from the counter. Marge was yelling at us to stop and Annie was wriggling her way towards us, waving a huge ladle.

'Yelp!' said Dave cheerfully, snatching his harmonica off the table. 'We haven't got time to argue. Let's split, folks!' Grabbing my hand, he raced me towards the door, with the others neck and neck, laughing his head off as Annie tried to dodge the tables and reach us.

Still high on the music, I almost fell down the stairs and out into the car-park, racing across the wide open space with the others until we collapsed, gasping, against the side of a battered van.

Then Christie looked at his watch. 'Right. Time to go.'

Job unlocked the back doors of the van and I thumped down to earth again as if someone had chopped my legs off.

'Have a good gig.' I backed slowly away from them. 'Thanks for the song.'

Christie looked at me. 'Why not come along?' he said softly. 'Just for the ride.'

'Great!' Dave clapped me on the shoulders. 'Jump in.'

After all those years I'd day-dreamed of taking off like that, I nearly chickened. It's the first thing every girl learns, isn't it? Don't Go Off With Strange Men In Cars. However big you are, however muscular, you always have to have that in a corner of your mind.

'We're O.K.,' Rollo said earnestly. 'Honest. We're not rapists or anything, and we'll run you home afterwards, won't we Job?'

'Sure.' Job shrugged. 'Anything. Just *get in.*'

Dave was tugging at my hand and Rollo was grinning hopefully. I looked across at Christie and I met that taunting stare again, daring me. *What the hell,* I thought. What was so great at home that I had to jump on my bike and pedal back to it like a good little girl?

'O.K.,' I said. And I climbed into the back of the van with Rollo and Dave.

Chapter 2

I would never have gone, not in a million years, if I'd known where they were going. When Job said *the gig*, I thought he meant somewhere dark and anonymous, a pub or a club where I could lurk around in a corner and ignore everything except the music. For the first half-hour of the journey I went on thinking that, while I sat jammed in among the drums in the back of the van, listening to Rollo telling me all their life histories.

Then, all at once, the van lurched and bumped and something—branches?—scraped across the roof. I sat up with a jerk and peered forward. A while back, when I wasn't really noticing, we had come off the motorway and I had no idea where we were now. But the road was rough and bumpy and it was very dark. Dark and quiet.

'Here!' My voice went shrill on me. 'What's up? I thought we were going to a gig.'

From the darkness of the front seat, Christie laughed briefly. But it was Job who answered my question, as calmly as though he hadn't noticed the shrillness.

'Sure we're going to a gig. Nearly there, in fact. I'm just trying to find the right house.'

'House? What sort of a gig is that?'

'Eighteenth birthday party.' Job was still peering through the windscreen. *'Darling* Chloe nagged *dear* Daddy—who's as rich as a chocolate sandwich—into letting her have a live band. Because she fancies Dave.'

'Naturally.' Next to me, in the back of the van, Dave stretched his long legs and purred. 'Who wouldn't? I'm so bee-oo-tee-ful.'

'Modest, too,' Job said shortly. 'Shy and retiring.'

'Of course,' Dave crooned. 'But mostly just *irresistible.*'

I hardly heard them. I was busy swallowing what Job had said. We were going to some vile party where everyone would be older and richer and snootier than me. *And I was wearing my school uniform.*

O.K., sure, it sounds a feeble problem. Since that evening, I've worn all sorts of weird clothes, and today I could walk into the House of Commons in a nappy and never turn a hair. But *then*—well, I was crippled by the idea of going into a strange, hostile place in my navy blue. It made me look, and feel, like a giant retarded freak even when I *was* at school. *I can't do it,* I thought.

At exactly that moment, Job said, 'Bingo! There it is. Foxes Lea. Puke and double-puke. What a delicious rural name!' He swung the wheel and the van crunched up a short drive and stopped outside a house that was even worse than I had imagined. Bigger and richer, with a great sweep of lawn in front, guarded from the road by a dark hedge. The lawn was landscaped with weeping willows and a lily-pond and artfully lit by hidden green lamps.

'Hal*lo!*' A girl—it could only have been Darling Chloe—came bombing out of the house, fair hair swinging, and flung herself at the van. She was small and slim and glossy, the kind of girl who looks as though she's spent weeks grooming herself and is just off to begin on her horse. The kind of girl you particularly hate when you're five foot eleven and twelve stone and wearing school uniform. She wrenched open the passenger door, chattering away in a classy drawl and calling to Dave over Christie's head. Then she yelled over her shoulder. 'It's them! They're here!'

The whole place went berserk, with glossy Chloe-clones, male and female, erupting from the house and whinnying round the van, trying to help with unloading the equipment. And there was Dave, showing off his muscles to the girls by carrying three times as much as anyone else, and Job, looking faintly sickened, and Rollo (as usual) being pathetically friendly to everyone. Even to the geriatrics who peered round the front door, who must have been

Dear Daddy and Dear Mummy. Everything was hectic and fast and noisy, swirling round me as I crouched in a corner of the van.

But after about fifteen minutes everything suddenly cleared and went quiet. The Chloes and the rest of the band trooped inside to set up and there was Christie, all on his own, standing at the back of the van staring in at me.

'Well?' he said.

I glowered at him. 'Think I'm going in there? You need a brain operation.'

'What's wrong?' His voice was innocent enough, but not the laugh that went with it. He knew I was scared all right.

I neighed. 'Can you see me cantering round with all those prime young fillies? I think I'll just stay in the van and munch my nosebag.'

'I don't want you to canter round with them,' he said, not even smiling. 'I want you to spit in their eye. Now get out and let's see what you're wearing under that mac.'

That made my spine crawl. Was he psychic? I stayed where I was. 'I'm wearing my high-tech chain-link aluminium track suit, of course. What's it got to do with you?'

'I don't chat,' Christie said coldly. 'You're the girl with the band so what you look like matters. Now get out.'

I shrugged and slid out of the van, waiting for him to jeer when I took off my mac. But he just looked me briskly up and down and said, 'Thank God. I thought you might be wearing something *pretty.*' His voice made prettiness sound like an obscene disease.

'Can you imagine what I look like in frills?' I said. 'I always go to parties in my school uniform.'

'It's fine.' He squinted up at my face for a second. 'Get the shirt off and just wear the jumper with the sleeves rolled up. And I think you'll be better with bare feet.'

'Anything else?' I said. 'Like me to black a few teeth?'

'You've got to fit in with the band,' Christie said and this time it sank in properly. He wasn't teasing or taunting me. He wasn't thinking about my feelings at all. All he wanted was for me to look right with the band. Feeling oddly flattered, I stopped arguing and began to take off my socks and shoes, shoving the spare things into the van. At least my hair was dry. I pushed it up and ran my fingers through it, trying to separate the tangled ends and make it softer round my face.

Christie had walked away from me, across the grass, while I was taking off my shirt. When I turned, he was crouched beside the lily-pond with a couple of empty paper cups out of the van.

'What are you up to?' I padded over to him, the grass feeling cold and clammy under my feet.

'Finishing your costume,' he said, quite seriously, signalling to me to bend down. Squatting beside him, I peered into the lurid, green-lit water and, too quickly for me to react in time, he turned and tipped water all over my head.

'You—!!' In an instant I was up, towering over him, dripping and furious.

'You look better without fiddly hair,' he said, standing up. 'Now come on, let's get in there.'

Lobbing the empty cups into the middle of the pond, he made off, without bothering to see if I would follow. I nearly didn't. Now I wasn't just wearing school uniform. I was bare-foot and furious and dripping wet as well. And Christie hadn't even waited for me. Serve him right if I stayed in the van after all.

Being miserable by myself.

Not bothering him at all.

O.K., so I'm thick. I'd be quicker now, but it took me a good ten seconds to work out that Christie wouldn't give a toss if I stayed and sulked. If I wanted to go, it had to be on his terms.

I'm not so dumb as to sulk when nobody cares. Running across the grass towards the house, I caught him up in the doorway, so that our reflections appeared together in the long mirror on the far side of the hall. Two angry, defiant images. Almost brutal. For a second, the shock of it stopped my breath. *I look like him. Ugly.*

Then my mind did a somersault and, all at once, I felt as

light as air, floating free as a balloon when the sandbags are thrown out. Looking your absolute worst is a sort of liberation. You've escaped from the game. The snooty Chloes could sneer all they liked now. It didn't matter, because I wasn't playing.

But of course they didn't sneer at all. They eyed me for a bit and then, once the party got going, they kept prancing up and whinnying at me, offering me glasses of wine and hunks of pizza and more glasses of wine. I even got a couple of invitations to join in, but the last thing Christie had said, before he picked up the mike, was, 'You don't dance,' and that suited me fine. I just sat in my corner and drank my glasses of wine and listened to the band.

I don't think I've ever seen anyone start a set the way they did. Christie blew down the microphone once and then glared out over the room, waiting for silence. He got it, too. The chatter died away and all the heads turned until the whole room was waiting for what he would say. When it came, it was only a single word, the name of the band, flung into the silence.

'Kelp!'

Then they were into the first song.

I know what you're expecting now. The day-dream version in the song. But Job never asked me what I felt before he wrote 'Face It' and he got it wrong. I wasn't stunned and ecstatic and swept off my feet. Actually, I was faintly disappointed. The band made a good enough noise and almost everything that you would expect was there: the contrast between Job's electronic keyboards and Dave's folksy solo instruments; the crisp rhythms of Rollo's drums; Christie's extraordinary voice. Even then they refused to sing anything except Job's songs and the risky, experimental feel of the band was already established. They didn't have 'Break-out' or 'Streatham Nights', of course, but they had 'Coming Good' and 'Living Over the Shop' and 'Supernova'. And yet. . . .

Somehow the whole effect was cold and complicated. Oh sure, I could see it was clever, but Christie had got me keyed up to expect something more. I wanted to feel a lump in my throat and get prickles on the surface of my skin. I wanted the singing to match the excitement of being in the café and staring into Christie's eyes and singing 'Down and Out'. And it didn't. That jam session in the café had been ragged and sketchy, but it had had *it*—whatever *it* was—and this clever stuff hadn't got it.

I didn't guess, though. When Christie finally leaned over, sometime after midnight, and said, 'What's your name?' I never even suspected.

'Janis.' I mumbled it through a sort of haze of wine and cigarette smoke. It seemed crazy that he hadn't asked before. 'Janis Mary.'

'Tough luck.' He pulled a face. 'What's your surname?'

I told him and he signalled to me to get up and come across to the mike. I guessed then, of course, not being utterly dumb, but it was too late to argue. Gripping my elbow, he pulled me forward to stand beside him and announced, 'Now we're going to give you a taste of Finch.'

The Chloes were very well brought up and they pulled their faces into kind shapes, but you could read their thoughts behind the kindness. *Let's be polite to the girl, as long as it's only one song.* If there's one thing I can't stand, it's being patronized. I don't remember feeling nervous. Only angry and confident, and unsteady from the wine. Those glossy faces were like a challenge and, without bothering to glance at the band, I launched into 'Down and Out', just as I had in the café, leaving Christie and the others to come in any old how.

If it had been planned, it probably wouldn't have worked again, but I was so full of wine and rage that nothing was going to stop me and this time I was ready when Christie joined in. We leapt above the tune and let our voices rise, sparring and swapping notes like a couple of wrestlers locked together.

For the first time in my life, I felt that miraculous change in an audience. It can't be seen or smelt or measured, but it fills the air like the tension before a thunderstorm, lifting you higher and higher and carrying you to places you never thought you could reach. It doesn't matter if it's an audience of Chloes or East End kids or old-age pensioners. As long as the music lasts, they're in your power, following every note.

It was magic. For about a minute. Then the room started to lurch about in front of my eyes and my stomach jerked into my bottom ribs, chopping off the word I was singing. Out of a strange jumble of faces and voices, Christie frowned at me, Rollo shouted above the sound of the drums and all the Chloes stared. Then I was away, pushing bodies aside, shaking off people's hands and ignoring questions, desperate to get out of the room.

I just made it through the front door. Then I was sick, very neatly, on the grass in front of the lily-pond.

The next thing I remember is waking up in the morning with Mum shaking my shoulder and yelling at me about school and trouble and how wicked I was. She sounded loud and fierce, but there was a tell-tale squeak in her voice and in spite of my fuzzy head and the pain behind my eyes I knew what that meant. Last night had scared the wits out of her and now she was letting off steam, straight into my ear, hot enough to scald my brain.

'How could you get into a state like that? And not even phoning. I was almost ready to call the police.'

A year before, I could have dealt with her, easily. I just used to put my arms round her and hug her so hard that she couldn't move. In the end, she'd calm down and cry on my shoulder and once that was out of the way we could talk things over sensibly. But now there was Himmler. I could see him peering round the door looking Deeply Grieved, and there was no way I was going to risk shedding a tear while he was around. I put the pillow over my head, but I could still hear Mum going on and on.

'That nice boy who brought you home was nearly crying he was so apologetic.' (Had to be Rollo. Only Rollo could bring a girl home late and drunk and leave her mother thinking how nice he was.) 'What must he have *thought?*'

I didn't give a pig's ear what any of them thought. All I

wanted to do was forget the band, forget the whole evening—and forget the sharp mental picture I had of the pool of vomit trickling into the lily-pond.

That feeling took ten days to wear off. Ten days I spent ramming the memory down into my subconscious and jerking sickeningly every time I glimpsed someone who looked like one of the band. If Christie or Rollo or Dave or Job had shown up in that time I would have run off down the street at full speed. Especially if it was Christie.

On the eleventh day I woke up from a dream about singing with Christie and almost cried because I'd loused everything up. If I'd only had the sense to realize how much I was drinking and lay off the wine, things could have been fantastic and maybe I would have had the chance to sing like that again. Now I never would, but the memory of the singing had taken all the flavour out of everything else. What little flavour there was.

On the twelfth day I dragged out of school with my mac undone and my case bumping my knees and there was Christie. He was leaning against the gatepost and watching the hordes file by, ignoring the curious stares he got.

'Hi,' he said, while I was still looking stupid. 'I brought you this.'

'What—? I mean, how did you—?'

He didn't bother to listen to my stuttering. He just pushed something into my hand and turned to walk away.

'Christie!' Behind me I heard a couple of girls giggle. Ha ha. Comic sight. Big Jan Finch running up the road after a skinny guy two inches shorter. I knew the jokes they'd be making, but there wasn't time to worry about that. Catching up with Christie, I grabbed his arm. 'What's up? Where are you staying?'

'Nowhere.' He kept walking, pulling me after him

because I wouldn't let go. 'I just came to bring you that and now I've got to get back or I'll miss my train.'

'But—'

He tugged his arm free. 'Play it and see what happens. There's no point in talking until you've done that.' He began to run and there was no way I could chase him again so I stood there like an idiot, feeling cheated and stunned and so happy that it choked me. He had come all the way from London just to see me for a couple of minutes. I had no idea what it meant, but for the first time in twelve days I could feel the air skimming the surface of my skin and my blood moving through my arteries. It was only when I had watched him run all the way up the road and round the corner that I looked down at what he had given me. A plain black cassette, without a label.

Chapter 3

'Hallo, Jan. Had a good day?'

Mum always called like that, and usually it was the best sound of the day. I'd make a cup of tea and we'd sit and swap stories of what we'd been up to, just like old times. Often I would go on chatting until Himmler's pallid face appeared in the doorway at half-past five and finished it—bang.

But that day I couldn't bear to wait to find out what was on the cassette. I suppose once upon a time I would have brought the tape recorder down and played it in the kitchen, for her to listen. But not now.

'Fine!' I yelled. 'Got a lot of homework, though.' And I made for the stairs without even looking into the living-room to see her.

She came out into the hall and called up after me, sounding puzzled. 'There was a boy asking for you. Wanted to know where the school was.'

'Yeah,' I said. 'Just someone I know.' Then I was safely into my bedroom with the door shut, leaving her to go on wondering, without any answers to her questions.

I didn't even bother to take off my mac. Just slid the cassette into the tape-recorder, plugged in the headphones and turned on.

There was a long, silent lead-in and then a jumbled snippet of drumming followed by whispers and distant, louder voices. What—? But before I could press a button or adjust the volume everything went quiet and Christie's voice grated clearly into my ear.

'Now we're going to give you a taste of Finch.'

And then straight into the song.

'Down *and out!*
Baby, when I found you I was
Down *and out. . . .'*

It was a hopelessly, laughably ragged start, with me ploughing in on my own before the boys were ready and Dave starting on the harmonica and then changing his mind and switching to guitar. And, of course, it wasn't a smooth, polished recording like a demo tape done in a studio. It was just one of the rough recordings Job did at most of the band's gigs. But, in spite of all those things, something came across.

Once we were going properly, it actually sounded the way I had felt while I was singing. Incredible. Usually when you do something that feels great, especially if you're drunk, the recording proves it was as exciting as lumpy blancmange. But this had a lift of its own, a charge that made me hold my breath.

While it lasted. But after a minute it finished with a jolt in the middle of a word and there was a noise of scuffling and running feet that made me cringe. Then silence again. I was just reaching out to switch off, disappointed, when Christie's voice spoke out of the silence, coming not from the huge space of a big room full of people but from somewhere small, like my bedroom. He might almost have been sitting beside me on the bed.

'Sounds good to me. I reckon we could work up something special if you decided to pitch in with the band. But think it over properly first. We haven't got any time for second thoughts once you're with us. If you want to come, you'll find us at 117b Ponders Lane in Streatham. You can have a week to make your mind up and then we'll write you off if we haven't heard from you.'

That was all and then it ended. No more details, no attempts to persuade me—not even a goodbye. I ran the tape right to the end and then turned it over and listened to the whole of the other side, but there wasn't another word, or another note.

What a crazy invitation. Did they really expect me to

take off and join them when I'd only met them once? Did they think I was the sort to run away to London like those idiots who sleep on the streets and get raped and mugged and hooked on drugs? I shoved the cassette into the very bottom of my underwear drawer and made myself start on my Maths homework.

After two problems I took it out and played it again.

The third problem took half an hour, because I kept getting up and walking round the bedroom, trying to clear my head so that I could concentrate.

The fourth problem never got finished at all. I sat staring at the tape-recorder and wondering, *What if I did go?* And then—worse—*What if I don't?*

Any idiot with half a brain could have seen that I wasn't going to do any good at school. Ever since I was twelve, I'd been fighting them, until even the Games staff and the Music staff were sick of me. No chance of Janis Mary suddenly coming good and stunning the world by getting twenty O levels. I was just working out my time and everyone knew it except Mum and Himmler.

And as for leaving and getting a job—hah!

But there, on that badly-recorded tape, was something I could do. I could do it as well as anyone I'd ever heard, and I was being offered the chance to take it up. Oh sure, I wondered if they were putting me on. But the train fare from London to Birmingham would make it an expensive joke and I didn't think I needed to be afraid of anything worse than a joke. People don't try to mess around with you much when you're my size, and they'd brought me back safely enough when I was drunk and incapable.

No, it was *crazy*. However straight they were. We might hate each other, we might starve to death and anyway I hadn't got a penny to pay my fare. Himmler and Mum would hardly give me the money or their blessing. Forget it, Janis. No train to dream-land this week.

That was the way the balance was tipping when I went down to my tea. A bit of friendly chat, a little less aggro from Himmler and I'd probably be in Birmingham at this moment, standing in the dole queue filing my nails.

But as I sat down in front of my pork chop Himmler said, 'Glad to see you could take time off from all that homework.'

Prod prod. Nag nag. So she'd been moaning to him about me, had she? I scowled and cut the meat off the bone.

'Finished, have you? Or will you be up in your room all the evening?'

Typical Himmler question. He didn't really want to know. He was just making sure I couldn't come downstairs to watch the television without admitting I'd been lying. I just shrugged and went on chewing.

'That's a pity,' Mum said. 'We're going out for a drink, and you could have come if you'd finished.'

I think she really *was* sorry, that she couldn't see how neatly Himmler had cut me out of their little treat. But sometimes it was hard to believe she was just thick and not purposely siding with him.

I gave her a look and went on eating my meal.

It wasn't until the front door actually clicked shut after them that I realized what day it was. Monday. I mean, I knew it was Monday, but I suddenly got what that *meant*, and it hit me so hard that I had to sit down on the bottom stair.

Over the week-end, Mum went round and collected up the catalogue money from all her customers.

On Monday she made out the papers.

On Tuesday, when she went shopping, she went to the bank and paid the money in. Which meant that on Monday night the money was all sitting in the house.

I'm not talking about ten or fifteen pounds, either. Mum really built up that agency when we were on our own, because we needed the money. There would probably be a hundred and fifty or two hundred pounds in the kitchen drawer, which was more than enough to see me to London and keep me for a week or two until I had time to suss o[illegible]
the situation. [illegible] ed and I

I began to tremble so hard that my t[illegible] that money
felt sick. There was nothing h[illegible]

except my own will-power. Oh, it would be lousy to take it, but Mum had a bit stashed away now that Himmler was around. She could easily replace a hundred pounds or so and it wouldn't take her long to save it up again without me to keep. Only, of course, I couldn't steal from her.

I can still feel what happened next. My brain was firmly fixed on not taking the money. I had definitely decided to leave it lying exactly where it was. But my body got up, as if it was acting all by itself, and walked into the kitchen. With my mind looking on, like a sort of neutral observer, my hands opened the drawer, took out the brown envelope which held the paying-in book and slid the money out from between the pages.

There was a hundred and seventy-three pounds and fifty-five pence.

I don't think I've ever been so scared. Not when our plane crash-landed in Glasgow. Not even when the fans went berserk in Melbourne. That moment in the kitchen, with the money under my hand, was the most terrifying moment of my life. While the money was ready to slip back into the envelope, I was still in the ordinary world, looking out at a lunatic day-dream of London and singing and Christie. Wild and impossible. But if I kept the money in my hand and put the envelope back into the drawer, then I had stepped into the day-dream and flung everything else away.

I took a hundred pounds and put the rest back in the book in the envelope in the drawer. Mum wouldn't discover she was short until she actually got to the bank, and I'd probably be in London by then.

The song's not exactly wrong, you see. There *was* a day when I ran away and left everything behind. But it wasn't that romantic, dark Wednesday when I met the band in the [illegible]way café. It was a wet Tuesday a fortnight later. I didn[illegible] came dow[illegible] dramatically in a blazing rage, either. Just [illegible]fast as if it was an ordinary morning, with my school-bag full of jumpers and jeans and a hundred pounds in my pocket.

Himmler spent the whole of breakfast going on at me about the results of my last Maths test and didn't I realize that that was one of the two subjects I had to have and really I was quite good at Maths if only I'd try and—I sat and ate my muesli and tried to look sulky so they wouldn't suspect, but all the time I was thinking, *In twenty minutes I'll be free.* The only bad bit was when Mum kissed me goodbye. I ducked away as quickly as I could and made myself remember how much happier she would be all on her own with Himmler, with no growling daughter to spoil the fairy story.

I'd forced myself to wait until I was my usual five minutes late and I lounged out of the door with both of them yelling at me to get a move on while I gritted my teeth to stop myself running. The air was cold and damp and puddles blinked up at me all along the pavement. There were the normal morning noises—cars, milkmen, children's voices—but they were happening behind a wall of glass. On my side of that wall there was only me, Janis Mary Finch, walking through the clear air.

I bought *Sounds* and *Smash Hits* and *Rockwise* to read on the train and all the way to London I turned the pages over and over until my fingers were black with ink and my eyes ached from staring at the photos of Michael Jackson and the free poster of Lionel Fram. But I never took in a word. It was as though none of it was really happening to me. Murderers or muggers or policemen would get me before I reached the band. Mum would magically guess where I was and take a taxi all the way to London to catch me. Mum—

But I couldn't think about Mum. There was no point in letting her into my mind again until I could send back the money with a note to say, *I've made it. Now you can be proud of me.* Squashing her picture out of my mind I tried to plan what I was going to do when I got to London, knowing all the time that it would never happen, that the train would never reach Euston.

But it did, of course. And there I was walking up a horrible grey, wet road in Streatham, feeling an idiot because there was no sign of the tidy block of flats I'd imagined, with its balconies and big windows.

117b was over a Chinese takeaway. Beside the shop was a door labelled *Flats only*. The catch was broken and it fell open when I touched it, showing a dirty staircase littered with empty takeaway cartons and smelling of cats. I checked the address three times before I rang the bell for Flat B. Nothing happened, but I wasn't really surprised because I was still behind my glass wall. I hadn't spoken a word to anyone since I left home and the silence wrapped me like a spell. In that queer mood, it was easy to walk up the smelly stairs, lumping my school-bag in one hand. After all, it didn't really matter what I did, because I must be mad. There couldn't really be a band called Kelp. I must have imagined the evening with them. And even if it was true, they were sure to have forgotten me. And anyway, they would be out.

They were in.

I knocked with my knuckles on the flat door and Rollo opened it almost immediately. Instant grin, all over his face. He swung back, ushering me in with a cheerful yell and a great wave of his arm and I ought to have relaxed at once, but it wasn't enough. It wasn't him I'd come for. As I walked in, I was so nervous that I could hardly breathe—which was just as well.

I've described that flat in a hundred interviews until it sounds the most exciting two-rooms-and-a-bog that ever sat on top of a cheap chow mein joint. The stack of baked bean tins and lager cans standing four foot high in one corner. The carefully selected records in the rack by the record-player and the camping stove Christie used to melt the rejects. The obscene cartoons spray-painted on the walls and the ceiling. Food and music and art and beer. Do-as-you-please partyland where life was one long high and no one bothered to open the curtains and let in the depression outside.

You want the truth? It *stank*.

It smelt so bad I actually took a step back when the reek hit me, before my nose went numb. Old cigarettes and stale cabbage leaves. Beer from the cans and meths from the stove, and feet. Especially feet. There were heaps of dirty washing next to the food and drink and most of the floor in the main room was covered with ancient, rotting mattresses. Job and Dave lounged side by side on one of them, waving beer cans and grinning, and Rollo flopped down on another, patting the space next to him.

The only person who wasn't flopped out was Christie. He sat cross-legged on the third mattress, very straight-backed and still and separate as a cat from all the mess, staring at me. I walked across the room awkwardly, clutching my bag, and waited for him to say something. The others were waiting too. The whole room was so thick with waiting that you could have chewed it and it began to stifle me as I stood in front of Christie, wanting some kind of sign from him.

Then, suddenly, I saw how I must look. Big Janis Finch, lumpy and pathetic, waiting for a nice polite welcome. Cucumber sandwiches and fresh linen towels in the guest-room. *Infantile.* I chucked my bag on the floor, picked up a can of beer and ripped off the ring-pull. Then I sat down on the mattress beside Christie and took a long, tepid drink.

He almost smiled.

'Hi, Finch. You took your time coming.'

A life in the day of ...

Finch

Janis Mary Finch—better known simply as Finch—has been lead singer of the band Kelp for under a year. In that time, they have leapt from being an obscure group, working a circuit of pubs and clubs, to being the heroes of the biggest pop success story for twenty years. Interview by Alison Jarvis. Photograph by J. Barleycorn.

I suppose people have this mental picture of bands that they lie around smoking all day and just leap up in the evening and switch on full blast for a few hours to go on-stage. I guess that's the idea I had too, before I joined Kelp. I wasn't so stupid I didn't know bands have to rehearse, but I thought rehearsals would be like jam sessions, with voices soaring and drums rattling and magic guitar licks appearing out of nowhere.

It may be like that for other bands, but you can scrub those ideas out of your head as far as we're concerned. We can't have a totally regular pattern, of course, because everything's bound to get thrown out by gigs and recordings and photo sessions, but basically Kelp operates on an iron schedule of constant hard graft with a bit of torture thrown in.

I turn up at the flat at 8.30 am. Sharp. The other four still live there, although they're making plans to move out now. I make the coffee while Christie kicks Rollo and Dave and Job into the new day. While they're falling into their clothes they moan and grumble and drink about five cups of coffee, but somehow we're always ready to go by nine o'clock.

The next hour is torture. We look back at the work we did the day before and pull it to pieces. If we've done a gig, there'll be a rough recording to run through, because Job always takes a tape unless it's impossible, but even without a tape there's never any shortage of holes to pick or complaints to make. It's the roughest time of the day. We argue and swear at each other without caring about anyone's feelings and we're all still feeble because we've just woken up. But it's a good way to begin the day because things can only get better after that.

At ten o'clock we get down to rehearsing. The worst sort—all the little bits. A couple of bars here and a line or two there. Maybe trying out a riff on harmonica (that's Dave, of course) instead of keyboards (Job) or guitar (Dave again). We spend quite a lot of time trying to make Rollo more daring. The drumming's all there, in his head, but he has to be nagged. We usually have two hours of fiddly rehearsing like that. Sometimes we manage to bully Christie into letting us have a coffee break around eleven, but mostly it's a steady grind, with Christie pushing us every minute.

'I think we even sweat music'

Smack on twelve, when the shop downstairs opens, Mr Liu begins bawling up at us, with threats of eviction and Triads and chop-suey through the windows if we don't shut up. That's one thing that hasn't shown any signs of changing since we struck lucky. Mr Liu still thinks we're a crowd of lazy no-hopers who never do any work.

From twelve to two, we eat. It's breakfast, lunch and dinner all rolled into one, I guess. Quite often, in the past, it was the only proper food we had all day. Rollo cooked it on the gas ring out in the back room and it was probably what saved us all from scurvy and beriberi. He had a huge pot and he chucked in all sorts of stuff: left-overs he'd cadged off the Lius, cheap veg he and Dave bought in the market on Saturdays and lugged home in nets, bacon scraps—even the odd sausage or two. It wasn't exactly cordon bleu—Dave was always moaning about starvation and making us feel his biceps to see if they were wasting—but it only cost about ten pence a day and it kept us going through Christie's killer schedule. Now we can afford it, of course, we have food brought in, but it's not the same.

The meal's still the best bit of the day though. We relax and ➤

fantasize about what's coming up for us. Rollo raves about amazing percussion instruments he's going to get. Drums from Africa and India and South America. Bells and cymbals and a great golden gong. Dave day-dreams about girls and I suppose I go on about things like oriental weapons. Even Job, who never really wants *things*, pretends to have cravings for silk shirts or vintage cars or crazy things like that. Christie's the odd one, as you might guess, the one who just sits and watches us all.

The time from two onwards looks as though it's always going to be chaos now. Journalists and photo-calls and all the rubbish that goes with PR. Like this interview. But basically, when we can get the time, we'll follow the old schedule we've always had. Light out from the flat and go off somewhere to do full rehearsals.

It's easy now, of course. We just go up and use one of Zombie's rehearsal rooms. But it was a real problem before. Not everyone wants a rock band belting out sets in their back room. People would take us in for a bit and then give us the push when the complaints started, so the pattern shifted all the time. But the one that was going when I joined the band will give you a general idea:

Monday. The day the chip shops shut. The one where Rollo's mum worked let us use their back room. Rollo's mum organized that for us by herself. She's a real star.

Tuesday and Thursday. We had a church hall, free, courtesy of the vicar. He gave us all the creeps, peering round the door when we were in full swing and flashing his whiter-than-white false teeth at us. We were always waiting for delicate little questions about when we were going to start coming to church, but they never came. Actually, I think we'd got the poor guy wrong. I think he was only trying to help, and he got a fair bit of stick from the congregation for letting us have the hall without paying. We had to turn out if anyone else booked it, which mucked up our plans sometimes, but Christie kept us going there because it was our best place. The only one with a stage and a reasonable sized room. We used it for flat-out rehearsals and for practising setting up and taking down. Christie's got this thing about how we always ought to look super-professional.

Wednesday. For some reason we never got anywhere very good, in spite of its being early closing day. Anyway, it's always been a funny day, because I have a karate class at one-thirty. We used to cut out rehearsals on Wednesday usually and do something like visiting our agent.

Gloom and doom, that was. He was a little grey man with asthma and he was terrified of Christie. I think he scrabbled up any old gigs for us just to keep us out of his office—Saturday nights in tough pubs, to fill in until the aggro started, and smelly basement clubs on a Monday evening when there was no one there. The sort of gigs where they just want you to play cover versions of the Top Twenty and they shuffle their feet and look bored if you try anything different.

The others were always on at Christie to ditch Frankie and get another agent, just like they kept nagging at him to make a demo tape and send it round the record companies. But he always said, *We're not ready yet*. All around us, bands we knew kept getting recording contracts and making a single or two and we wanted to copy them, but Christie just pointed out that the records vanished without a trace. He went on saying, *Not yet* and trudging back to Frankie. I don't think we finally got free of him until Mae came along.

Friday. That was a good day. Rollo's mum's neighbour went to the hairdresser and Rollo's mum let us have her lounge. Lousy acoustics, but a smashing free tea and NO HASSLE.

Saturday and Sunday were hopeless for rehearsal space. If we were lucky, we were off up the motorway to a good gig. Otherwise we sat round and discussed our stage show, dead serious, as if we were playing the Albert Hall instead of Little Piddlington Annual Youth Club Dance and places like that. Quite often on a Saturday, Rollo would pick up a bit of work with the Lius, helping out in the kitchen to stretch our disastrous finances a bit further. Come to think of it, Mr Liu was really good to us in those days, without making a song and dance about it. We didn't earn *quite* enough to live on from our gigs, but we did too much work for the boys to be able to sign on. And I couldn't, of course, because in the beginning I should really still have been at school. If it hadn't been for Mr Liu, I guess we might have been starved into selling off the van, once or twice. And that would have been the end.

Nowadays, weekends are the worst scrum of all. It's lovely to get out and play live, of course—a band like Kelp can't survive without it—but it's great when we have time to go round to Rollo's mum's for one of her fantastic high teas, the way we used to.

Whatever we get up to in the afternoon, we knock off by six at the latest, and much earlier if we're going to a gig. Even now, though, there's usually a couple of evenings a week when there's nothing to do. We stop in at Mr Liu's for some ➤

fried rice—double helpings if he loves us and the scrapings from the wok if he thinks we're getting above ourselves. Then we annoy him by hanging round the shop to watch TV. The only day we streak upstairs is Monday. On Mondays, wherever we are, we always turn on Radio One and listen to Rat Saunders at seven o'clock. Oh yes, even now. I mean, the Rat's compulsory listening, isn't he?

And that's it. No wild parties. No stunning night-life. On the evenings when we're not playing anywhere, we often go to bed around ten-thirty, to make up for the three and four o'clock in the morning sessions and the long drives home in the early hours.

It's not a soft life. On top of all that, Job's writing songs, sometimes at the rate of two or three a week, Rollo and Dave are fitting in instrumental practice of their own and I have to do karate exercises every day. I guess we're probably tense and over-tired a lot of the time, but the music keeps driving us. We eat it, we breathe it—I think we even sweat music. Whenever we're tempted to slacken off and settle for second-best, Christie's always there to force us on. That's how it's always been. Right from the moment I joined the band. ■

The Sunday Times Magazine

Chapter 4

I hadn't got a clue what I was walking into, that first day. Before I could properly catch my breath or finish my can of beer, we were up and away to rehearse in the church hall. I can still see us now. The four of them setting up, practised and professional, and me ploughing in like a stupid puppy with its tail wagging.

Like a stupid puppy that gets its head smacked.

'Come on, let me help. I'm good at heaving things around. What can I do, Christie?'

'Nothing.' He didn't even look round at me.

'But I can't just sit and watch you all working—'

He did turn then, sharp and irritated. 'Yes you can. And you will. Get yourself into a chair and keep your mouth shut for the next three hours.'

Three hours? If he thought I was taking that, he was dreaming. Marching forward until I was only a foot or two from his face, I glared down at him. 'I came here to *sing*. Not to gawp at you lot. If you want a groupie, I'm going home and you can find someone else.'

'You'd never make the grade as a groupie,' Christie said coolly, looking me up and down. At that range, it was like being fingered, unenthusiastically, and Dave's snigger didn't help.

'Look, we're rehearsing for tonight's gig,' Rollo said, blundering in, trying to spare my feelings. 'We can't fit you in just like that. It's got to be worked out, Finch—'

He was the one who got it in the neck. Poor Rollo. I whipped round and snapped at him, even though it wasn't his fault I was angry.

'That's another thing. Who the hell d'you think you're

calling Finch? A finch is a *bird.* My name is Janis, and that's what you're going to call me, or—'

Christie stepped back and punched me hard on the jaw. It took me by surprise and I went straight down, feeling an idiot while he stood over me and frowned.

'Right. Get this. While you're in the band, you're called Finch. Because I say so. And you don't sing a note until you've listened and got the sound of the band into your blood. Now shut up and sit down and stop wasting valuable time.'

I looked up sulkily. 'How long until I get to sing?'

'How do I know? Probably a fortnight or so.'

That took my breath away all over again, but it was too late to argue. Christie was already away up on the stage, testing the mike. Rollo would have helped me to my feet, but the others called impatiently and he left me, with an embarrassed, apologetic shrug.

Rubbing my jaw, I crawled into a chair half-way down the hall. *You'd never make the grade as a groupie . . . you don't sing a note until you've listened . . . probably a fortnight . . .* I was sore in so many places that I didn't know which to think about first.

I guess I missed a couple of songs, because I was too busy with pretending I didn't care, but even then Kelp wasn't a band you could ignore for long. They weren't rehearsing at full volume—that's a crazy, exhausting thing to do—but even with the amps turned down they get inside your head. Without Darling Chloe's wine to muffle my brain, I heard the real strangeness of the music, the sharp contrast between Job's eerily sweet melodies and Christie's harsh voice. Let's face it, with most of the songs around you could fill in the rest when you've heard the first couple of lines. But not Job's. You have to keep listening to them. I still thought there was something missing somewhere, but sitting in that empty, cold church hall I got the hang of the music properly for the first time. Understood that it was edgy and different and memorable. With all that discussion and rehearsal, the band had a smoothness, a style that other groups never get. It was like the difference between real silk and nylon. It's difficult to describe, but you could feel it instantly. I got so deep in that when the vicar peered round the door, giving me his toothy grin, I glared at him until he ran away.

It was around five when Christie looked at his watch and stepped back from the mike.

'Time.'

At once, the four of them slid into the routine for striking the set-up. Five minutes it took them, and I was so ignorant, not having seen how other bands blunder about, that I wasn't even impressed. Just sat there and wondered what gig we were going to.

Poor, dumb Janis.

Christie nodded at me as he jumped down from the stage with an armful of neatly coiled leads. 'Come on. We'll drop you off on the way.'

So I wasn't even going to the gig? Well, I learn fast, especially with a sore jaw to help me, and I didn't waste energy wingeing about it this time. Just fixed Christie with an iceberg stare.

'I'm not a parcel.'

He smiled. Oh, I know, you've read it a million times in tatty paperbacks. *He smiled at me and my knees turned to water and I.* . . . Well, for God's sake, how *do* you describe that feeling? I clutched my battered school-bag and forced my face to keep frowning.

'You're going to be a parcel *bomb,'* Christie said softly. 'When you go off, you'll hit the audiences harder than anything they've ever known. O.K? You'll only take the edge off it if you hang round the band beforehand.'

'A *time* bomb,' murmured Job to himself, always being one for the right word. And Rollo and Dave nodded enthusiastically, so there could be no doubt they were all on Christie's side.

I may be as dumb as a haystack, but I got the message. All the time I was afraid they'd forgotten all about me, they must have been discussing me, getting everything sewn up behind my back. Without giving me a chance to put my oar in. I suppose I should have stamped out in a fury or forced them to tell me the lot, there and then, but all I could think was, *They want me* and I just grinned like a size sixteen idiot.

'It's going to be worth waiting for,' Christie said. 'The first performance of the *whole* band.' He grinned again, fiercely, and lifted his head, his body going taut. 'What's it going to be?'

The others shouted back cheerfully, as if it was a ritual they knew. 'It's going to be perfect!'

'*What's* it going to be?' Christie said again, leaning towards me.

I could hardly speak the word. 'Perfect.'

But perfection's a tomorrow thing. Today is always make-do-and-mend and that's how that day finished. Still grinning stupidly, I piled into the van with the rest of them, expecting to be dropped off at the flat and busily deciding to spend the evening playing all their records. Instead, Christie hauled me out in front of a mean-looking house round the back of the shops.

'What—?'

'This is where you're staying, for the time being. Got your bag?'

I stopped dead, straight-legged and straining backwards, like a dog pulling against a leash. 'Oh no I'm not.' How meek did he think I was going to be? 'If I'm in the band. I'm living in the flat with the rest of you.'

'If you slob round the flat all day and all night,' Christie said shortly, 'you'll wind up either frustrated or pregnant. It would be messy and wasteful and bad for the band.' He took out a key and unlocked the front door. 'So you stay here. Right? Just to keep a bit of space between you and the others.'

I noticed he left himself out, but I was almost too angry to speak. All I could trust myself to say was, 'What house is this, anyway?'

'My mum's.'

It was more of a shock than a mere surprise and before I

had time to digest it he had poked his head round the door, yelled, 'The girl's here. The one I warned you about,' and turned to sprint back to the van.

'Hey!' I shouted.

The only reply I got was from Job, who waved a slow hand and called, 'See you tomorrow.'

So there I was, all on my own in front of a strange house, staring into a small, cluttered hall.

Christie's *mother?* My mind dreamed up monsters as I stood there waiting for her to appear. A great eighteen-stone momma, who would engulf me—yes, even me—in a huge bear hug and tell me how she *adored* Christie's friends. . . . A clever, sarcastic mother, six foot tall and skinny as a dry stick, who would look me up and down and ask me if I had any O levels. . . . A red-haired *femme fatale* with a husky voice. . . . A Lesbian feminist. . . .

But nobody came at all.

The house was still and silent except for the sound of a television from the back room. Like son like mother, I thought. I could stand there all night waiting for the Great Welcome. Crossing the hall in three strides, I made for the T.V. noise.

'Mrs Joyce?' I stepped into the room as I said it.

'Mmm?' She looked round, not like any of my monsters. Small, blank and very, very grey.

Oh sure, her hair was brown and her eyes were blue and all that stuff, but she was utterly *nothing,* like a fluff ball under your bed. As if she'd run down years ago and no one had ever cared enough to wind her up again. She stared vaguely at me and I thought, *Perhaps strangers wander in and out all the time.*

'I'm Janis Finch. Christie said you were expecting me and—'

Oh brilliant, Janis. Ten out of ten for perception. This woman hasn't expected anything for years. She's forgotten how to do it and lost the instructions.

But I went on standing there, because it's difficult to do anything else in a strange house unless you've come to mug the cat. After a bit, the woman sighed, made a huge effort and spoke to me in a zombie female version of Christie's voice. Same metallic tone, but an octave higher and without any of the energy and aggro.

'Oh yes . . .it's upstairs . . the little front bedroom . . . but I haven't had time to hoover or . . . you can go up if you like. . . .' The sentences got away from her before she could finish them and she turned back to the television.

Then I understood. I may not have any O levels, but I'm well qualified to recognize depression, after what I went through with Mum. There was no point in hanging around waiting for this woman to perk up. I'd have to take care of myself. Without bothering about excuses, I lugged my bag out of the room again and went to explore upstairs.

There were two bedrooms at the front. I opened the door of the left-hand one and shut it again, fast. It was a classier tip then the boys' flat—stank of scent instead of beer and old socks—but give me the choice and I knew which I'd prefer. Female slumminess makes me puke. Torn tights and bits of cotton wool and talcum powder on the floor. *Eugh!* She had dirty frills and tatty 'feminine touches' everywhere as well. The night-dress case—with the night-dress tumbled on top of it—had *Ida* embroidered in flowing script and there was a grubby pierrot doll in the chair.

The other bedroom was O.K. by comparison. Not exactly a millionaire's day-dream of course, and too small for anyone except a dwarf, but there was a bed and a wardrobe and nothing worse than dust in the corners. I managed to shove a window open and let in a bit of air from the street outside, where a couple of scabby starlings were quarrelling over a crust. Home, sweet, sweet punishment cell. Oh well, at least it was a place to lay my bag.

I laid it and then, being nosy, went out on to the landing and tried the door of the big bedroom at the back. But although I pushed at it as hard as I could I couldn't budge the door and I guessed it must be locked. Ridiculously, I fixed on the idea that it was Christie's room. That if only I could see inside I could begin to understand him. Turning the handle, I pushed the door one last time, but it still didn't shift and I had to abandon it.

Then, at long last, starvation hit me. Breakfast had been my only meal of the day and, quite suddenly, I thought I'd collapse if I didn't get something, but I didn't fancy the notion of discussing menus with Ida downstairs. Instead, I went back to my room and got my purse. I reckoned I could sneak out for fish and chips and leave the door on the latch. The house was hardly a burglar's dream and old Ida would be perfectly safe until I got back. Even if someone did get in and beat her up, she would never notice.

Chapter 5

I really laid into Christie when he finally turned up, the next afternoon. All day I'd been waiting not liking to go round to the flat in case I missed them and furious at being left on my own. And I hadn't come all the way to London to get saddled with someone *else's* droopy mother.

'She's *sick*. You could wheel in a squadron of gorillas to do square dancing and she'd just look round once and turn back to the T.V. You ought to do something about her.'

'She's O.K.,' Christie said unemotionally, putting the van into gear.

'Oh sure. Bubbling over with fun and games. Ho ho hoing like Father Christmas, isn't she?'

'What do you want me to do? Stand over her and wipe her nose?' There was a snap to his voice now. 'She's got pills from the doctor. You don't need to fuss with her.'

'But—'

'Shut up.' He spun the wheel fiercely, to take us into a side road and backed into a minute parking space. 'Out.'

'What *now?*' We weren't at the flat or the church hall or anywhere I recognized.

Christie smiled his cobra smile. 'We're stopping off at the barber's. Turn left at the end of the road.'

Wow. Real fun time. I'd waited all day and now I was going to have a treat and be allowed to watch Christie having his hair cut. Couldn't he have done that before he picked me up? It hardly looked urgent, anyway, but I was getting wary of raging at him. He stayed so calm that I was likely to be a physical wreck before his pulsebeat rose at all. Better to follow him to the barber's and say nothing.

It was a pretty depressing place. Clean enough, but dull

and small. It was a real shock to go in and find it crowded out with kids having their hair done. Christie ignored the receptionist and the girls at the front doing tints and cuts and went straight to the back of the shop.

'Jed!'

'It's my tea-break!' roared a voice from behind a curtain.

'It's Christie,' Christie said. For some reason, that had an effect. Jed peered round the curtain and looked us both up and down.

'Must have been bloody drunk.'

'Course you were,' Christie said. 'Pissed out of your mind. But you'll do it, all the same.'

'Yeah?' Jed pushed the curtain out of his way. He was massive—so massive that I felt like the Sugar Plum Fairy standing beside him. His face was red, his hair was red, even the bristles up his nose were red. 'Why should I? Just give me one good reason, Joyce.'

'Because the band's got to have the best,' Christie said calmly. 'And you're the best.'

It didn't seem much of an answer to me, but Jed snorted and shambled into the shop.

'This is Finch.' Christie pushed me forward and Jed nodded and gave me a brief, sharp look.

'Hi Finch. Have a seat.' Picking one up with two fingers, he spun it round so that it was facing away from the mirrors and waved me into it as if we were making a social call. Then he looked at Christie, over my head. 'So? What do you want?'

'Not for me to say,' said Christie. 'You're the expert. And you know the band.'

Jed looked down at me again and even *then* I didn't get it. Not even with them standing one on each side of me, peering down. I just wondered why Christie didn't sit down in a chair and let Jed start snipping.

'Well?' Christie said after a moment.

Jed snorted again. 'Got to be a Block, hasn't it? With that face. It'll be *cream.*'

'O.K.' Christie nodded. 'You can have twenty minutes.'

'Do us a favour!'

'Twenty minutes. Then we've got to go.' Christie said.

He stood beside me, with his arms folded, and as Jed picked up the comb and scissors Janis Finch, Genius of the Year and All-Round Brain, finally got what was going on. I jerked sideways, only just missing the points of the scissors with my ear. The kids in the shop were already staring at us and I kept my voice low, hissing at Christie.

'Don't bother asking me! How about tattooing my nose while you're at it? Or engraving nursery rhymes on my teeth?'

'Be quiet,' Christie said. 'Stop wasting time.'

But Jed looked doubtful. 'Here, Christie, I thought you'd talked it over with her. She might not like—'

'She'll like.' Christie put a hand on my shoulder to keep me in the chair. 'Because it'll be right for the band.'

'Oh yeah?' I glared up at Jed. 'Fancy being sued for assault, do you? Just you try touching me with those scissors.'

The kids were gawping now, all right. Even the other stylists had stopped working and were flapping their ears. But Christie ignored them all. He came round to the front of the chair and put his hand roughly underneath my chin, tilting it up so that I had to look him in the eye. 'Let's get this straight right now. I'm not playing kids' games. The band is a serious working band, and if you're not prepared to treat it like that, you can get the next train home.' There was nothing jolly about his voice, not a touch of teasing. The look in his eye froze me into silence.

After a minute, he looked up and nodded at Jed. 'O.K. You can start now.'

And Jed did. He didn't look wild with joy—I guess there really are laws against forcible hair-cutting—but he laid straight into my precious long, thick hair, the only bit of me I liked. And there wasn't any of the friendly chatter you get from your local barber down the High Street. He went at it with fierce concentration, stepping back every now and again to look at the damage and then closing in with flared nostrils breathing hard and scissors going full pelt. It was like being scalped by an Aberdeen Angus bull and mostly I just kept my eyes shut and my fingers crossed. I didn't fancy my chances of getting out of there without losing an eyebrow and half an ear.

There wasn't a hope of seeing what was happening, with the mirror behind me and Christie's stony, unreadable face in front, but locks of hair were falling like icicles in a thaw and unfamiliar draughts caught my scalp in queer places. The girls at school who fussed over their hair always made me laugh with their agonies every time it was cut, as if it would never grow again, but whatever Jed was doing to me seemed fairly Attila the Hun. I could feel flutters of panic starting.

Then suddenly, without any warning, he flung down the scissors, rubbed his hands together and nodded. Christie, who had watched every snip in total silence, looked me up and down and then nodded back.

'*Double* cream. That's what I wanted.'

It seemed as though everyone in the shop knew what I looked like, except me. Glaring at Christie, I stood up and turned round to see the worst.

I've got enough self control not to shriek at shocks, but I nearly bit off my tongue keeping the noise back. No prizes for guessing why the cut was called a Block. My head was clipped short and square, like a yew hedge made to imitate a box. On a little, bony girl it might have been great, probably made her look fragile and vulnerable and all that corny rubbish, but it just turned me into a thug. I looked brutal, like a hefty gorilla with a bald face.

I made sure it was a blank face, though. Christie and Jed were watching me, waiting for my reactions and work hadn't started in the rest of the shop either. Well, they could just go on guessing. What I think of my body is private. I held the blank expression for thirty seconds or so before I got the right scornful, sarcastic voice to comment.

'It's a knock-out. What's it for?'

'What's the matter?' Christie said. 'Did you want to look *pretty?*'

I didn't see how anyone could want to be as stupendously *un*pretty as Jed had made me, but that was my business. I grunted.

'It's a knock-out, like I said. Wild. But it'll need cutting every week. I'm not sure I can afford the overheads.'

'Jed'll take care of that. He does all of us, because he's our original fan.' Christie prodded me in the ribs. 'You might say thank you. He's not cheap, you know. South of the river he's King, and he's done you proud.'

'Great, Jed,' I said. Not sarcastically this time, because it really was a stylish, skilful haircut. For anyone who wanted to look like a gorilla with a bald face. I gave him a grin to show I meant it and then I went, fast, avoiding eyes all the way to the door. I had to get away from those mirrors.

Christie obviously didn't realize that I was speechless as we got into the van. When we'd been travelling for a couple of minutes, he looked curiously at me.

'Don't you want to know where we're going?'

I snorted. 'To have my left ear amputated? Or my nose curled?'

He ignored the heavy humour. 'You're going to find out how I could knock you over so easily yesterday.'

'Oh?' Shows you the impression he'd made on me. I was taller and broader than he was, but that knock-down had seemed perfectly natural to me. 'Where *are* we going, then?'

'A dojo I know.'

'O.K. show-off.' I leaned back and stared through the windscreen. 'If you're not telling, I'm not asking.'

'Sure I'm telling.' He whipped through a set of traffic-lights, at the last possible second before they changed, and treated me to a quick, mind-bending smile. 'I just wanted to get your reaction. See if you knew anything about martial arts already.'

I shut my eyes. 'Am I crazy or am I crazy? I run away from home to sing with a band and the next thing I know I'm up to my neck in haircuts and karate. What's going on?'

'Being in a band's not just singing, you know. It's a

whole image, a way of facing the world and putting yourself across, on-stage and off. I'm setting you up so that you add to Kelp's image instead of weakening it.'

I swallowed that one as he parked the car again. This time we headed for a dingy pub on a street corner. The pub was closed, of course, but Christie took me to a door round the back and led the way up a narrow staircase, pushing open a door at the top.

I guess the dojo was once a boxing gym, but most of the exercise junk had gone and there was a big, empty room with a couple of punch-bags up one end and a rack of martial arts magazines. Bernard was sitting cross-legged in the middle of the floor, reading a newspaper. Christie nudged me.

'Bow.'

'*What?*'

'Just ordinary politeness.' He bent forward from the hips and then went inside, kicking off his shoes just before he crossed the threshold. I felt an idiot copying him, but it didn't matter what I felt like, because no one was watching me. Bernard had stood up at the first sound of Christie's voice and was walking down the room towards him, with an odd expression on his face.

He's a skinny, oldish guy, in his early fifties, with as much Japanese in his face as you get from one grandparent and a lifetime of pretending it was all four. The Welsh lilt in his voice is a real shock the first time you hear it and I couldn't even identify it until Christie told me he grew up in Cardiff.

'Come back at last have you, Christie? What is it, then? Going to beg a few free sessions to get back into training?'

'Something like that,' Christie said. 'Meet Finch.'

He dragged me forward and I wondered, for a split second, if there was some strange oriental ritual I ought to know about. Perhaps I should kneel and put my forehead on the ground or pull a humble, modest face? I settled for sticking out one hand and saying, 'Hi.'

That seemed to be O.K. Bernard gave me the long stare

he uses on strangers and then nodded. But he spoke to Christie, not to me.

'So? Girl-friend? Sparring partner?'

'She's in the band,' Christie said, 'and her voice is fine, but she needs to learn to move.'

'And I'm going to teach her?' Bernard blew a raspberry. 'How long is it, Christie? Four years? Five? And you think you can walk in here and start asking favours? Forget it. I might have managed something for *you*, because you used to be worth it when you were fifteen, but not for anyone else.'

'Oh, I'm still worth it,' murmured Christie. 'I haven't forgotten just because I don't come here any more.' Reaching into the big pocket of his parka, he pulled out a short, thick stick, black and glossy. 'Remember this nunchaku? You gave it to me when I won that competition, when I was thirteen.'

It all sounded very casual. Christie wasn't even watching Bernard; he was looking at a sparrow on the sill outside the window. But something seemed to tighten in the air of the room. Bernard stared at the nunchaku. 'I remember.'

Christie glanced over his shoulder at me. 'Look, Finch.'

With a twist of his hands, he unscrewed the stick. It came apart at the middle, where the metal band was, and fell into two halves, joined by a short, strong chain. Christie grinned and began to whirl it at arm's length and it gathered speed, hissing faintly as it swished through the air. I found that I was clenching my fists, waiting for the moment when he would lash out at something. But he didn't. Instead he gradually let it slow down and grinned at Bernard.

'Don't be so tight. This is important to me,' he said. 'It won't kill you to help me out.'

Suddenly it was embarrassing to be standing there watching them. Nothing was going to be spelt out, but a blind, deaf idiot could have told what was going on. There was some feeling there, something long-standing and emotional, and Christie was deliberately playing on it. No trickery, you understand. I could tell from Bernard's expression that he knew he was being manipulated and I watched him swallow it and let himself be hooked.

'Suppose I'll have to give in, won't I, if I want any peace? I know you, Christie. You'll be round here nagging me every day and twice on Sundays until I say yes. But the girl had better be a quick learner. I'm not wasting months on her.'

'Oh, she won't need a proper course,' Christie said lightly, looking at the sparrow again. 'Just a few *katas* she can use on stage and perhaps a bit of *tameshiwari.*'

Bernard looked shocked and angry, as though Christie had spat in his eye. 'Like me to throw in a bit of ballet as well? And a drop of weight-lifting?'

'*It's what she needs.*' Christie whipped round, suddenly fierce and dead serious. 'I can see her, in my mind, and I know exactly how she fits into the band, but I can't teach her everything myself. I *need* you to do it, Bernard.'

It took almost half a minute, but in the end Bernard shrugged and said, 'It's prostitution,' in a voice that meant, *Oh all right, I suppose so.* It was months before I understood what was holding him back, before I understood that karate is a whole, balanced system and not a bag of tricks that you can dip into to pull out what you want. But even then, in my ignorance, I got the main message of that little scene. The band was what mattered to Christie. He had the whole thing in his head, like a blueprint, and he would use all his energies—and everyone else's energies as well—to make that blueprint real. And now I was a part of that.

It's great. Great, I kept saying to myself as we made polite goodbyes to Bernard and went down to the van again. *Free room, free haircuts, free karate lessons—what more could any girl want?* Common sense told me to shut up and let Christie get on with things, if that was the price of being in the band.

Only common sense never alters how you feel, and I was feeling blacker and more furious by the minute. I thought I'd run away to escape from being pushed around and it looked like I was going to be worse off than before.

I finally blew up when we reached the flat. We were going up the stairs when Christie said, 'Now let's have a beer while I tell you what you're going to need to wear on stage.'

That did it. I really let rip. 'And what else after *that?* Hey? You're too fond of treading on people's faces, Christie Joyce. It's time you took your foot out of my mouth and let me say what *I* think.'

'No point,' Christie said calmly. 'You don't know enough about the band to say anything worth listening to.'

'How am I supposed to *if you won't let me sing?*'

'All in good time.' He tapped on the door of the flat and as Rollo opened it I could see all the others inside, staring at my hair. That did it.

'*My* good time,' I yelled, 'not yours. I'm going back to my room now, and I'll give you lot twenty-four hours to decide that I can begin singing. After that, I'm off to Birmingham.'

Turning my back on them all, I stamped down the stairs and out into the street, frantically thinking, *I've blown it, I've really blown it now.* No feet hurried after me and no one called, but they might have been watching me from the window. I went with my head held up, walking briskly all the way to Christie's mum's. That was one good thing about old Ida. At least she wouldn't interfere with me. I could leave her to her depression and get on with my own in peace.

It took me five minutes of hammering on the door to get her to let me in. And then, of course, she goggled at my new, sensational appearance. It might even have shocked her into speaking to me, if I'd let it, but I wasn't about to start on that.

'Janis?' she squeaked, like a neurotic mouse. But I grunted and pushed my way past, thundering up to my bedroom before she could squeeze out another word. I had to do some hard thinking. How was I going to cope if my ultimatum went wrong?

Half an hour later, my floor was littered with bits of paper from my notebook.

Dear Mum,
Perhaps you're surprised to hear from me like this, but I want to say I'm sorry. I was wrong. I thought you'd be better off without me and I could get by on my own, but. . . .

Hi Mum!
This is your wicked daughter, writing to you from the Big Apple, to say. . . .

Dear Mum.
Please try to understand. . . .

It was no use. However I wrote it, it wasn't a letter I was ever going to finish. Oh, I could have got across what I wanted to say if I'd just been writing to Mum. Even if I couldn't find the exact words, I could have trusted her to understand. But each time, after the first couple of sentences, my mind clogged up with a picture of the face that would be peering over her shoulder. She had no secrets from Himmler, and whatever I wrote he would read as well. I could imagine him gloating over poor little down-and-out Janis, relishing the prospect of giving her a pat on the head and a ton of interfering advice. And once I'd written he would know from the postmark that I was in London, and he might even come to track me down.

Well, he wasn't going to get the chance. By the time I'd crumpled up half a dozen letters, I knew that I could never go back there. I couldn't even write. Not until I'd succeeded and I could pay Mum back that money and thumb my nose at Himmler. But I couldn't go back to the flat and apologise to the band either.

They had to come to me.

Chapter 6

It took the whole twenty-four hours. I'd more or less given up—I was even beginning to throw my clothes back into my bag—when I heard the hammering at the front door. My feet moved automatically, three steps, and then I came to my senses. No use making a dramatic stand and then running downstairs like a three-year-old as soon as someone comes. Play it cool.

Play it Finch. The words came into my head by themselves, and I grinned as if I'd overheard a joke. O.K. that's what I'd do. Christie had invented this tough, strong person called Finch and perhaps it was time he learned that he couldn't push her around. Janis Mary was pretty soft, but Finch made a great disguise.

After a couple of minutes, Ida roused herself enough to open the front door and I heard feet climbing the stairs. I had my coat on and my bag in my hand when the knock came. 'Yeah?' I said, in a carefully bored voice.

Stupid of me to think it could have been Christie. He would have let himself in with his key, of course. But I wasn't prepared for anyone else, and I was thrown by the sight of Rollo standing in the doorway, smiling nervously.

'Can I come in?'

'O.K.' I shrugged and sat down on the bed. 'Well?'

He blinked at me. 'We want you to come back. Of course.'

I stiffened my mouth, to keep the grin under control. 'Oh yes? And when do I get to sing?'

He beamed, like a kid presenting a gigantic bouquet. 'How would tomorrow suit you?'

'That's better,' I said. 'I suppose.'

'And you will?' He looked quite anxious. For two pence I could have patted him on the head.

'I might. If things are going to be different. Christie'll have to start treating me a bit better.'

'But of course he will.' Rollo sounded surprised. 'He was only—' His mouth shut—snap!—but I was on to him at once. I'd already sussed Rollo out. Look him straight in the eyes and there was no way he could bluster or tell you a lie. So I gave him the full treatment. A solemn wide-eyed stare with just a touch of nervousness. Pure Janis Mary.

'He was only what? Oh look, it's not fair to expect me to decide about things if I don't know what's going on. Is it, Rollo?'

He went a beautiful strawberry pink and the words came tumbling out. 'Come on. You *must* have guessed Christie was winding you up on purpose.'

'On *purpose?* You mean he *wanted* me to lose my temper?'

Rollo wriggled like a little kid caught out chalking rude messages on the blackboard. 'That's what we all liked about you in the beginning. The way you spat back at Christie. Stuck out your chin and opened your mouth and sang, in that lousy café, not giving a damn for anyone. But then—'

'Then I came to London.' Yes, I could imagine it. Me standing meekly in the flat, gripping my bag and waiting to be bossed around. 'You must have thought I was pathetic.'

'Oh no. No.' Rollo went even pinker. 'It's just that—well, we thought you would ask questions. Make conditions. Complain about the way we'd sent for you. When you didn't, we were afraid that what you'd done in the café was just a fluke. And then, when you went on taking what Christie said—'

So they'd been terrified that they'd landed themselves with a pallid, watery Janis Mary sort of person, had they? I stared down hard at my fingers, still gripping the handle of my bag, and thought about Finch, as hard as I could.

'It's really great, isn't it?' I said, when I could trust my voice to come out hard and fierce. 'Really fantastic, playing your little games with *people*. Suppose I'd caved in? Gone bananas and started chewing the stairs? You didn't know I was tough enough to take being pushed around and leaned on like that.'

'I—' That got him. The pink went pale and I thought, *Aha. Not* your *plan, was it?* You *hadn't worked out the risks*. But I was ready to bet that Christie had.

'It was O.K. though, wasn't it?' Rollo said quickly. 'You came up just the way we'd hoped. Strong and hard.'

Inside my head, a crazy little character was rolling round screaming with hysterical laughter, clutching her stomach and kicking at the walls. Strong? Hard? It was wild. Just at the moment when I was feeling about as tough as a cornflake in the rain, in comes Rollo and sets me up as Finch the Super-Hero. Doing it so innocently and happily that I nearly fell into the goodwill trap and let him smooth over everything. But there was one more question I wanted answered before I settled for peace on earth.

'So why wait twenty-four hours before you came to get me?'

'Christie said we had to be sure you were serious. That you weren't just making a gesture that you'd abandon if it didn't work. We wanted—'

They wanted to see if I'd come crawling back. I didn't need it spelt out for me. I'd spent twenty-four hours chewing my finger-nails and feeling sick with panic about where I was going to go next, and it had all been manipulation. Well, watch out, Christie Joyce. The man who goads the tiger gets his balls bitten off. I think that moment, when I realized just how hard I needed to be, was the moment when I stepped into Finch's skin, for the first time.

It was also the moment Rollo chose to grab my hand. He squeezed it and muttered, 'You mustn't think we didn't like the way you were. I was really upset about your hair. I like long hair, and yours was beautiful.'

I stared at him, too surprised to say anything. He might just as well have been reading out a recipe for stuffed guppy fish for all it meant to me. For a second our two hands lay together on the bed, like something weird that happened by accident. Then Rollo got the message and bounced away from me so hard that he hit the headboard and made it twang.

'As long as you're not feeling . . . that you're out on your own. I mean we all think . . . that is. . . .'

There's no fun in hurting Rollo. It's much too easy and it shows too clearly on his face. I grabbed his hand back and gripped it between both mine.

'Thanks, Rollo. You're right, I do need a friend.'

That made him smile again, but we both knew I'd warned him off, delicately but definitely. He's probably the nicest, gentlest person I'll ever meet *and* he looks stunning *and* he's even taller than me. Janis Mary's dream. But I couldn't quite manage to take him seriously. Not with Christie soaked like a dark stain into my mind.

The end result, of course, was that I turned extra-friendly, by way of apology, and we ended up going off to the flat arm in arm, with all my aggro safely packed away until the next time it was needed.

It was only much later that it dawned on me that that was probably why Christie had sent Rollo, instead of coming himself.

But I wasn't exactly sharp about anything in the beginning. Once that little scene was over, for example, I thought everything would be chocolate candy. That I would instantly, magically, become a full member of the band, as though I had been there all the time. I imagined it like diving into a swimming-pool. Tottering for a second on the top board and then, with a sickening, curving leap, shooting through the air to splash gloriously over the head in music.

There was a great sickening, curving leap all right, as I launched into rehearsals—and then there I was, stuck in mid-air, getting goose pimples on my thighs.

In my ignorance, I'd thought that we had the new sound sewn up after those two short sessions, at the café and at

Darling Chloe's. I thought all I would have to do was join in with what the band was already singing and add my own special whatever-it-was to that. What I hadn't realized was that a band's not just four or five people playing together. It's a living thing, very finely balanced, and if you crash in and alter one part the whole lot's likely to come out in boils.

There was no way Kelp was suddenly going to start doing versions of songs like 'Down and Out', just to fit in with me, either. All their songs were written by Job, specially for Christie's voice, usually doubling that with one or other of Dave's solo instruments. (It's a pity Dave ever uses his mouth for talking. On the flute and the harmonica and the little tin whistle he's pure magic.) But then, out of the blue, there *I* was. They knew I could add something to the band, but they hadn't really got a clue how to work me in, not even Christie.

We tried having me sing in harmony with Christie, having us sing turn and turn about, having one singing the words while the other sang scat. But whatever we did, the songs limped like geriatric crocodiles. And the harder I listened to Christie and tried to fit in with him, the worse it got.

It reached boiling point on the Friday of the second week. We'd had an hour and a half's rehearsal at Rollo's mum's house and Christie had made us go over the same song nine times, trying different arrangements, each one worse than the last. As we finished the ninth, Rollo's mum looked round the door.

'Come on you lot. Tea's up in the kitchen.'

'Great. Thanks.' Christie nodded without turning round. 'We'll be there in a minute. I just want to try—'

'Christie!' Dave groaned, like a mummy rising from the tomb and Rollo looked tired and patient.

But it was Job who put a match to the bonfire. He stood up and said, 'No.' Quiet and very fierce. 'I'm not rehearsing another note. We're chewing up the songs and destroying the band, without getting anywhere. Either we go back to what we were, or you can look for another keyboard player.' He glanced across at me and smiled his wistful, washed-out smile. 'I know it's rough, Finch, but someone had to say it.'

'But we *did* get it right! In the beginning!' I bunched my fists and banged them on the arm of the chair. 'That first evening was magic. Double cream. There must be some way we can get that back and —'

'Just show us how,' Job said softly.

They were all staring. Rollo was miserable, Dave was impatient and Christie was as wary as ever, but I knew the look and I knew what they were thinking. They were all beginning to change their minds and think it would be better to get rid of me. As if I could jump on a train and go back home. Oh they thought I could still do that, but I wasn't going to disillusion them. Weeping on people's shoulders is definitely out when you look like me. There had to be another way.

'It's these endless rehearsals!' I said loudly. 'How do you expect me to be any good when I never get to do the real thing and sing at a gig? Why don't you give me a chance?'

'But you can't just—' said Dave.

'Why should we risk—' said Job.

'Oh Finch, how can we—' said Rollo.

All at the same time.

Christie looked thoughtful and when the other three had finished gibbering, he nodded at me.

'O.K. You just might be right. You can sing at both the gigs this week-end and if that doesn't work we'll chuck it in. Agreed?'

I nodded back, fast, before the rebellious look on Dave's face turned into words. 'Agreed.' But I felt so sick I could hardly eat any of Rollo's mum's beautiful gingerbread.

If I'm ever in danger of forgetting about stage fright, I remember that Saturday night's gig, imagining myself back to the smoky, crowded pub, with the boys setting up and me crouched in a corner trying to psyche myself up to produce a magic performance. In my mind, I ran through every song in the first set at least twice, trying to keep track of what arrangements we'd finally fixed on. And all the time, curious eyes were watching me. Dave had three girls buzzing round him, Jed was leaning against a wall talking to Christie and the landlord was frowning in my direction. All of them obviously knew it was my first time. When Christie called, 'You ready?' my stomach lurched like a rocket taking off as I went to join him at the microphone.

My whole life is hanging on this moment.

At a time like that, you can do without Great Thoughts. They louse up your breathing and take your mind off the audience. And with that particular audience, that was a recipe for disaster.

They weren't too bad at first. More puzzled than anything, because most of them knew the band and Christie launched us with the familiar 'Kelp!' as if nothing had changed. I think they were intrigued, though, and ready to be won over. If we'd started well, we would have had them where we wanted them.

But within ten minutes the scuffling had started as people stopped listening and turned away to talk. Once you've lost that first link, that thread of attention that ties the audience to you, you have to work up a thunderstorm to get it back. Your mind drags out idea after idea. Do we strip off? Stop singing and swear at the kids? Set fire to the stage? And all the time you have to keep going, churning the song out because you're being *paid* and the landlord, or the owner or the promoter is glaring at you from the side.

That night, I made the idiot's mistake, the real dumb beginner's goof. The more people shuffled and laughed and shouted, the faster I sang, dragging the rest of the band along with me. Turning a dull disaster into a hectic disaster.

The drums rattled behind me, the feet shuffled in front, heads turned and voices rumbled. As they got louder, so did I, until I was yelling, in an attempt to overtop everything, forgetting I was on the wrong side of the speakers. Round the other side, as I strained my throat and my lungs, the noise must have been appalling.

Then suddenly, on the other side of the bar, a hand shot out, throwing beer. A space cleared instantly, like snow under hot iron, leaving two boys in leather facing each other with their fists up. Bodies made a ring, shoulder to shoulder, and all the talking stopped.

And so did I.

It turns my stomach, even now, to think I could have been such a moron, chopping the song off in mid-note and gasping over the microphone, just to bring the drama home to everyone.

As if I'd given a signal, the two boys crashed together, viciously, one of them pulling a knife, and a second later that whole side of the pub erupted into a single huge fight, with everyone piling in.

It took an hour and six policemen to sort out the mess. Result: one broken jaw, one knife wound in the arm, six arrests and a cocktail of different blood groups.

And one lost gig.

We were lucky, really, because the publican actually paid our expenses, but his face was like a lemon as he counted out the money into Christie's hand.

'Don't bother coming back. If you can't keep the lads quiet any more, I've no use for you.'

No one answered. No one looked at me. Even in a situation like that, there's a hard core of loyalty, because a band is closer than a family. But as we were getting into the van, Job said bitterly, 'Three years we've had that gig. Every two months, regularly.'

I squeezed into the back and clenched my teeth.

Don't answer him.

Don't apologise.

And don't—don't you dare cry Finch, you stupid cow, because there's always tomorrow and then you'll make it work. You'll sing like a tornado so just don't snivel now—

In the dark Rollo patted my hand and I had to chew my bottom lip hard to keep from howling. Because I didn't really believe in tomorrow. I'd already given it everything I could and I knew the others were just waiting for me to let them off and back out of Sunday's gig.

But it was Finch they wanted, and Finch wasn't the sort of person who'd back out of anything.

All the way back through London, I swore silently at myself, gritting my teeth. By the time we reached Streatham, my jaw ached, but at least I hadn't made a fool of myself. I didn't crack until they had dropped me off and gone on to the flat.

But then I cracked all right. Oh sister, I cracked, like a wineglass dropped on to a concrete floor. As I unlocked the door, my face was already shaking and I was breathing in gulps of panic. Partly delayed shock, I suppose, but mostly the thought of the rest of my life to sort out. I only just got inside before I had to lean back against the door, swallowing tears and struggling for breath.

I swear I didn't make a sound, but as I stood there, with my arms wrapped round my body, a nervous face peered out of the sitting-room.

'Janis?'

'No!' Breaking my silence, I yelled full blast, uncontrollably. 'It's a six foot maniac with a cutlass and if you don't get back inside I'll have your guts—'

Charging for the stairs, I leaped up three at a time, still bellowing, and shut myself in my bedroom, ramming the bed up against the door. I didn't want Ida's twitchy face and big weepy eyes appearing round *that*. She should have left me alone. What did I care if she was hunched in front of the T.V. now, wailing her head off? She was Christie's mother, not mine. Let her wail.

Ten minutes later, there was a small tap at my door and then the sound of someone walking away without waiting for a reply. I had calmed down just enough to be curious. When I heaved the bed out of the way and opened the door, I found a mug of cocoa standing on the floor outside.

I *hate* cocoa.

But not drinking it would have been like stamping on a baby seal and life was so terrible that one cup of cocoa couldn't do much to make it worse. I sipped it numbly (sugar as well!) while I worked the songs over again in my mind, as though I didn't already know every note of every part. Over and over and over. . . .

Chapter 7

I didn't go up to Rollo's mum's for lunch the next day. Just shut myself up in my room and ate Mars bars. Half of me was hoping that the others wouldn't pick me up for that night's gig after all—and the other half was snarling because no one had looked in to collect me for lunch and I really needed a free meal. The only human voice I heard was Ida's. She shuffled up and down the landing a couple of times and then tapped at my door.

'Janis? I've cooked a few sausages. Would you like some?'

Cooked? First time I'd known her do more than butter a piece of bread. Alleluia. Haute Cuisine Blossoms in Streatham Back Streets. But it wasn't going to blossom in my bedroom. A cup of cocoa was enough encouragement for one week. I didn't even bother to reply.

She hovered for a moment or two then shuffled back along the landing. But she didn't go downstairs. I heard her open the door of the back bedroom and go inside. For perhaps a quarter of an hour, she was in there, moving slowly round and I nearly got up and took a look, because I still had no idea what was in there. But misery kills curiosity and I just couldn't work up the energy to get off the bed. I stayed there, working over the songs, dreading the moment when the van would arrive—and all set to go and smash up the flat if it never did arrive.

It came at five. No chat. No tender questions about my health. Christie stood at the bottom of the stairs and called up.

'You coming, Finch?'

I counted to three before I opened the door. 'Yeah, I'm coming.'

'Make it fast, then. We're in a hurry.'

Picking up my bag, I slouched down. As I reached the front door, a faint voice from the sitting-room said, 'Have a nice time. Good luck.'

'Been chatting up my mother, have you?' Christie sounded amused. 'Tea and scones in front of *Crossroads*? Gossip about knitting patterns?'

Shows you how low I was that I didn't even have the guts to jeer back at him. I just crawled into the van and said, 'Where are we going?'

'On to your home ground.' Job started the engine. 'Near Birmingham.'

'And it's one of the best gigs we've got,' Dave said roughly. 'We don't want you—'

'Belt up.' Rollo prodded him with a foot. 'Quit hassling her.'

The tension in the van was so strong that a moron could have guessed how they had spent the day. Arguing about me. If I'd been a nice girl—Sweet Janis She's Got Such A Lovely Nature—I would have pulled out then and there to spare everyone the agony of grinding through another failed gig. It would only have taken half a dozen words to change the atmosphere in the van to pure honey. But I needed a miracle more than any of them knew and I couldn't afford to give up my only chance, because there was no cosy home-coming for me afterwards. *Finch,* I thought, *Finch.* And I pulled her round me like a tigerskin to cover my trembling. I was determined to stay with the action. But I hoped we weren't going too near my part of Birmingham.

Rollo tried to chat, but that just made it more obvious that the others were ignoring me. And anyway, what was there to say? I was about to make my last appearance, and we all knew it. Retiring at sixteen, with no other kind of future and no place to go. I tried not to think about the next day as I skulked and glowered and grunted answers at Rollo.

And then we got to the gig—and it was Polo's. Not the greatest club in Birmingham, sure, but important enough for me to have heard of it from way over the other side. It was a fantastic gig for a band like Kelp and if they'd asked me nicely then I would have cleared off and left them to make the most of it. But all of them, even Dave, had obviously agreed to stick with their promise. No one said a word as we took the van round the back and looked for a place to unload.

Once we were out of the van, it was hopeless to try and discuss anything. Polo's speciality is having three different live bands every night, each playing three sets, so that the music goes on from nine to two at maximum energy, without a break. The club is a huge cellar with tiny stages in three corners and a bar in the fourth and the effect is sensational. *If* you can solve the acoustics problem before the crowds pile in.

By the time we got there—innocents on our first visit—the other two bands had the place staked out with their gear on the best stages. They were taking turns to do sound checks and they weren't wild about letting anyone else muscle in. It was hard to argue. The headline band was Silent Night and they were in an ugly mood. They couldn't afford minders in those days, but that was before the heroin got a real hold on Henty so they hardly needed them. The other lot were jokers called The Scarlet who pulled out our plugs when we tried to cut in on them.

We finally managed to scramble fifteen minutes sound time just before the club opened. Then we went upstairs to the poky dressing-room. By then, the bog was blocked up and there were six people clustered round the mirror doing their hair and plastering on make-up. Christie elbowed his way in and snapped 'Fast!' at us, over his shoulder. Being the real unknowns, we had the opening set and we'd got about ten minutes to change.

At least I could get by without the mirror, having no make-up to put on and no hair to speak of. I fought my way to the clearest corner, on the far side, and took my stage clothes out of my bag. When Christie had decided that karate uniform was not what he wanted, and conned a ninja suit out of Bernard, I'd hated the thing, but now, slipping it on, I felt that I was putting on armour. While I wore that rusty-black suit, I was Finch, the shadow warrior, capable of anything. Wriggling my feet into the soft *tabi* boots, with their separated big toe, I stood up and turned to look at the rest of the room. Perhaps, after a while, it would stop being peculiar to undress in front of strangers and I would be like Leila, the Silent Night drummer, who was lounging round in her bra and pants. Then I remembered that there would never be another time and I felt very cold as I bundled up my jeans and pushed them into my bag.

I was just sorting out the black hood that I wore until I began to sing when Polo looked round the door. He was like a sleek, overfed dog, jowled and paunchy, with a nasty, snappy temper.

'Anyone here called Janis Finch?'

I waved. 'Me.'

'Well get out here fast. There's a guy making a nuisance of himself. Says I'll regret it if you go on before he's spoken to you. I won't have trouble here. If you don't sort him out, you don't play.'

Dropping the hood, I made for the door. 'He's asking for me? But—'

But no one knew I was there except the band. A quick glance at them didn't help. Rollo and Job looked as surprised as I was, Dave was busy chatting up Leila and Christie was bent double, tying his shoelace.

'Got a groupie?' one of The Scarlet bellowed. 'Is he a giant or a masochist?'

'Sexist jargon!' Leila snapped, and they began to bicker as I struggled between them and out into the corridor.

Before I could scrape my wits together, a voice said, 'Janis?'

Himmler. Ginger bristles, pallid freckles and all.

If I'd been wearing the hood, which hides everything except my eyes, I would have tried to bluff it out, but as it was he had me dead to rights. While I was still catching my breath from the shock, he snatched my elbow and hauled me into a corner by the door of Polo's office, doing the full Grieved Parent bit.

'...you must be able to imagine how we felt. Your mother's been having nightmares about rape and drugs and dragging the river. Why couldn't you talk things over with us?'

His soggy eyes were soulful and he was puffing warm breath into my face to show that he was sincere. Onions for tea, I thought. And then wished I hadn't, because fried onions were what Mum cooked to cheer us up in the hard times. I turned my head away and reminded myself of the proper technique. Total silence and let him work himself up into a froth.

'You're only sixteen remember. I've got a right to make you come home.'

'Rubbish!' I couldn't keep it back. Not when he'd said that. 'You haven't got a right to make me do anything. You're not my father.'

Oh dumb, Janis, *dumb*. That gave him a peg to hang an answer on. And he used it. Worse than anything I expected. He gave a disgusting smirk and murmured, 'But it won't be long.'

'What—?' Then I got it. 'She's *marrying* you?'

He nodded smugly. 'Next week. I always wanted it, but your mother wouldn't agree. Not until you ran away. Then we talked it over and, from what you'd said, we thought you must be embarrassed about us. That it would be easier for you to come home if we—'

'She's marrying you to please me?' It was funny, it was hilarious, it was so side-splittingly ironic that I could hardly keep control of my face. 'If she's *that* concerned, why isn't she here herself?'

Himmler looked down at his finger-nails. 'Well—actually, she doesn't know you're here. It was me that took the phone call, and I thought it would be nice if I could get you back for the wedding and—'

'Ha ha!' I said sourly. 'All wrapped up in silver and blue paper like a wedding present, I suppose. You've got to be crazy. You wouldn't stand much chance of being a happily married little couple if I—'

Then I got it. I may be slow, but I can suss out some

pretty sinister things, given time. Of course Himmler didn't want me lousing up his neat cosy wedding. He wanted me out of the way as much as I wanted him out of the way, but he was too much of a hypocrite to admit it. This way, he could claim he had really tried to bring me back, if Mum ever found out about the phone call.

The phone call.

From the corner of my eye, I saw the boys walk out of the dressing-room and start going down the spiral iron staircase to the club.

'What phone call?' I said quickly.

Himmler smirked again. 'I don't know if—'

Grabbing his shoulder, I shook it, hard. 'Quickly! I have to go on now. *Who phoned?*'

He tried to look as though he wasn't enjoying the bad news. 'It was your friend Christie—Joyce, is that the name? Said he thought we might like to come and hear you sing, seeing you'd be so close—'

I felt my fingers go cold as ice. What a great plan. So that was why Christie had been happy to let me come along that night. Himmler was meant to carry me off neatly to save Christie playing the heavy chucker-out and upsetting Rollo and disrupting the band. Only Himmler wouldn't play. There I was in the middle, with two of them trying to push me off on to each other.

Well I wasn't going to be pushed! Who did Christie think he was, picking people out of nowhere and then dropping them again when they didn't work miracles? He wasn't going to get away with it this time. I knew now that I couldn't beat him up, with a few miserable karate lessons against his years of practice, but there were other ways of getting at Christie.

I shoved Himmler out of my way, so hard that he thudded against the office door and before I took another breath I was along the corridor and half-way down the stairs, erupting across the club just as Christie shouted 'Kelp!' Job played the opening bars of the first song as I raced towards the stage. Christie was on the far side, in front of the mike that he and I had been going to share.

Without pausing, I unclipped the mike from the stand and sailed over to the other side of the stage—two whole yards away—leaving Christie to share Dave's mike if he wanted one.

Right now, Christie Joyce! I'm going to ruin *this* gig on purpose!

I didn't wait, the way we'd rehearsed, for him to sing the verse and then let me filter into the chorus. No subtleties. I banged into the verse myself and magically, after all those careful, detailed rehearsals, the notes came just as I wanted them, so that I could let my anger spill over into the music. And the song took the anger and absorbed it, without bursting. Came over hard and strong and bitter.

Don't try to live by newspaper headlines
They're just out to get you.
Lie low instead, cover your head
And keep doing whatever you're told

I couldn't keep it up, of course, not after running all that way at top speed first. By the end of the verse I had to stop for breath, so that Christie got the chorus. He shocked me into attention by not raging back at me. By singing it absolutely deadpan, in a mechanically perfect voice, like a human synthesizer.

Save your breath
Don't speak unless you're spoken to
Don't step out of line
Save your breath

Then I was there again, but he kept with me for the second verse.

Pretence can keep you from falling
But keep it in your head
(he was making fun of me now, singing spiky arabesques over my line, like a terrier teasing a badger)

If you take it for real, They'll know how you feel
(that was too near the bone and I had to struggle with my voice)
And your fantasies will be laid bare

The rage and pain were turning me inside out. I left the chorus again and all the others sang it together, four-square, like an army on the march, taking their cue from Christie. Battering me back to home and Himmler and Mum in Himmler's arms. Depression and failure and the dead end of the line. I began the third verse light-headed, shutting my eyes and taking it slow, because it would be my swan song. The end. With nothing afterwards.

You can't change the way that things happen
Though your head tells you maybe you can
(and now there was nothing except my voice. Somehow—at a signal from Christie I guessed—everything else had stopped and I was out on my own, letting the lines take their natural pace, feeling the movement of them and hearing the notes flow out of me)
Even if you start trying, They won't stop lying
So keep doing whatever you're told

I opened my eyes and saw Christie. Apart from our stage, the whole club was dim and Christie's face swam on the edge of that dimness, looking pale and excited. *Christie excited?* For a moment I didn't get it, as though I had been somewhere far off, out of touch. And then it crystallized sharp, like ice, and Christie lifted on to the balls of his feet with his back taut and his hands clenched round the mike and I *knew,* I knew as if he had spoken, what he was going to do with the end of the song, which we had rehearsed very quiet and fading. As he opened his mouth and fired the first line at me, I was ready, spitting it back at full volume.

Save your breath
Don't speak unless you're spoken to
Don't shout unless you're shouted to
Don't sing unless you're sung to
Don't step out of line
Don't sing out of tune
Save your breath!

On the last word, I threw my microphone hard at his face, chopping the note off short as I caught him on the cheek-bone. *Christie Joyce I hate you I love you I can't bear you as close as that.* Then I was finished. Letting my head drop forward and my hands hang loose, I waited for the next thing to happen by itself. Rollo and Dave and Job were all staring at me and over the far side of the club the door opened momentarily and in the light from outside I saw a familiar freckled figure push his way in. Muzzily, I wondered who would attack me first.

For a moment the club was utterly silent and I realized that it had been like that before, while we were singing. Then people started to push their way to the bar and, as the ordinary hum began again, a voice spoke from just in front of me.

'You. Girl.'

I looked down 'Me?'

'You.' She was sharp-eyed and unselfconscious. Fifty if she was a day and built like a block of flats with cropped bronze hair and enormous glasses. As far out of place as Donald Duck on a grouse moor. 'I'm Mae Grierson and I want to talk business with all of you when you've finished this set.'

'You want—?'

'Business,' she said again, briskly. And then she grinned. 'I think you need a decent manager.'

. . . . 'Stanley? Me. . . . What do you mean what me? Me Mae, of course. Why are you so slow. What's going on there?. . . . Well, get a bath towel then!'

(Impatient foot-tapping.)

'At last! What were you doing? Weaving it yourself? Now listen, I want to take a gamble. . . . Oh, *much* worse then opening the Liverpool office. This is quite different.' (Deep breath) 'I've found a band. . . .

. . . What do you mean *what sort of band?* Would I be phoning you like this about a brass band? Or a rubber band? For Heaven's sake pay attention, Stanley. This is going to cost us a lot of money. . . . Of course it's going to make money in the end. . . . Of course I'm sure. Am I *ever* wrong? It's a fantastic investment, but we've got to leap in now, because Chas Larsen was having his usual nose round and even Polo was looking a bit beady. You don't get any chance for second thoughts in the music business. Remember Pauly Grant?. . . .

. . . . Of course I'll tell you. I'm telling you now. Why don't you *listen?'* (Pulling cross-eyed faces in Polo's office mirror.) 'I'd nearly sewn up the deal with Polo. Yes, he wants the whole club done, *and* the offices, *and* his own house as well. . . . Yes, I'm sure it's a fiddle, but it's not our worry, is it. We were getting down to the nitty-gritty when a weedy little guy with freckles came charging in, muttering about some girl in a band. You know what Polo's like. Can't stick with one idea if another comes along. So I let him go off to sort out the girl business while I poured myself a brandy. He'd only just come back when there was a *monumental* thud against the door. It flew open and in staggers the little ginger guy again. Really funny. Polo went purple and I decided I'd go down to the club and have a look at the troublesome girl. . . . Yes, of course I clinched the deal with Polo afterwards. I'm not a child, Stanley. Yes, he'll sign as soon as we send the papers. . . . STANLEY GRIERSON WILL YOU SHUT UP AND LISTEN TO ME! I'm trying to tell you about the band.

Their first song was a knock-out. The girl's concentrated danger, like a fist in the face, and the whole lot goes into her singing. . . .

. . . . No, of course she's not pretty. Pretty! Why don't you climb out of that cash register and look round the world? Is the Ayatollah pretty? Am *I* pretty? It's irrelevant, Stanley. It's energy and originality that count, and that power that slams you in the ribs. This girl's got them all. She's strong and she's got style and the tension between her and the other singer is fantastic. There's a kind of sexual charge. . . .

. . . . No, I'm not getting carried away. I've been on the edge of the music business for thirty years and I know what I'm talking about. . . . What do you mean have I been drinking? Of course I've been drinking. When did that ever make a difference to *me?*. . . Of course I'll let you handle the contracts. When I've persuaded the kids they need us to manage them. . . . Oh, I'll get them all right. Don't I always get what I want? . . .'

Chapter 8

She was—wait for it—an interior designer. In fact, she was *the* interior designer, a Total Environment Specialist whose patch ran from London to Liverpool, and her clients were famous and freaky, most of them in television or the music business. Polo was pretty small beer for Mae. Her speciality was transforming really plush clubs and never giving up on the smallest detail. If she needed a mid-Victorian bedpan with enamelled roses and blue-birds, she would find it, even if there were only five in the world.

And now it was us she was after.

But softly, softly. No fool, old Mae. Having chucked a hand-grenade into the middle of the band, she withdrew smartly, without another word, to let us carry on singing. And landed smack on Himmler's toe, just as he was slinking towards the stage. He apologized, of course—ooze, ooze, creep, creep—even though it was her fault. For some reason she seemed to take an interest in him and she whisked him off to a table before he could get at us. As we started singing again, I could see him with his elbows on the table, swigging his drink and gabbing away.

It would have put me off singing, even if there had been anything to be put off. But the thread between me and Christie had snapped at the end of 'Save Your Breath' and there was no way I was letting myself go under like that again. The rest of the songs went as we had rehearsed them, perfect and mechanical and dead, and the few people who were there that early began to shuffle and crowd round the bar. The set was just something we had to drag our way through.

When we finally stopped and the band in the opposite

corner started, two figures made for the stage. Himmler was close, but Polo was used to working his way round the dancers and between the tables and when he beckoned us we leapt off in his direction, all together, without even speaking.

'Janis!' Himmler croaked from behind us as we made for the stairs. 'Janis, I want to talk to you!'

Too thick-skinned to be embarrassed, he came bumbling along behind us and, as Polo shepherded us into his office, there was Himmler squeaking about outside, trying to follow us in.

But no on else got in. Not even Polo. There was only the band, standing in a huddle by the door, and Mae, sitting in Polo's chair drinking brandy and soda. She didn't offer us any and she didn't waste time on the social chat.

'That was lousy,' she said. 'All of it except the first song. What do you think you're up to?'

'Thank you so much,' Job murmured, for us all. 'Free advice is so welcome. Especially uninvited.'

'Well here's some more.' Mae drained her glass. 'If you can produce that first song again, the same way, turn up at Joe Busby's next Thursday. Three p.m. Philip Tissiman will be along to record a demo disc with you.'

No messing about. Splat. The top independent recording studios. The new up-and-coming record producer. All conjured up at no notice in half an hour on a Sunday evening. It was a fantastic demonstration of the sort of clout she carried. Rollo gasped like a little kid and Job whistled through his teeth, obviously impressed. I was too ignorant then to understand much, but I'd already worked out that it took a lot to impress Job. For a split second there was a fairy-tale feeling in the air. Cinderella, you *shall* go to the charts!

Then Christie said, 'We've got a gig on Thursday.' Very stiff and angry.

Mae put down her glass. 'Cancel it.'

'Why not just make the recording yourself?' said Christie. I still hadn't worked out what was wrong, but I could feel the others gathering behind him, just from habit, wiping the smiles off their faces, standing straighter and more aggressively.

'What's the matter?' Mae said. 'Got a hang-up about taking advice? If you don't listen to anyone else, you'd better listen to me, if you know what's good for you. My speciality is being right.'

'So is mine,' said Christie, too uptight to speak loudly. 'And Kelp is my band.'

He went for the door then, without another word, and we all followed him. As he opened it, there was Himmler outside, pallid and goggle-eyed. Christie shoved past, but Job gave him a wide smile of unbelievable sweetness and stepped aside, pulling him into the room. 'Why don't you talk to this lady here?' he crooned. 'While we get on with the serious discussion.'

Then we were outside, with the door slammed after us, before Himmler could give a single goldfishy gulp. Christie glared back towards the office.

'That would do wonders for our credibility, wouldn't it? Being managed by a ten ton grandmother.'

'Sexist and ageist,' murmured Job. '*And* weightist.' He looked down at his clenched hands. 'She was right, though. About the song.'

'Of course she was bloody right!' Christie said angrily. 'I'm going to the pub down the road until our next set. To take away the taste of that overbearing whale.'

And for a while that looked like the end of it. No one said another word about Mae as we sat crammed into a little smoky bar with one eye on our watches and the other on Christie's furious, silent face. Only Job, as we got up to go back to Polo's, muttered, 'Pity about missing Philip Tissiman.'

After our second set, Polo looked into the dressing-room and gave us a note.

Al Charlton, A & R man for Clogs Records, will look in at your session on Thursday. They're searching for a new band now Semaphore have split up.

Oh, and I got rid of Janis's stepfather. He saw that it was crazy to force her back home just when the band's about to make good. But I promised J. would write to her mo. so she must.

M. G.

'She pulls more strings than a harpist,' Christie said sourly as he tore the note into small pieces and scattered them on the floor.

The Scarlet put their beer cans down and stared.

'I like her technique, though,' said Job. 'And she's offering carrots at the moment, remember. Suppose she decides to get the stick out? That's a lot of clout to take on your backside.'

You've said it, I thought. Anyone who could get rid of Himmler like that was no feeble-minded old woman. Even if she had bought him off by promising the letter I couldn't write. Christie must be insane to keep pushing her away. But I couldn't say anything. Not when she'd picked out the one song I'd intended to ruin, the one song I'd snatched away from Christie, overturning all the careful arrangements. Anyway, we weren't likely to start on serious discussion of anything when we were crammed into that poky dressing-room, with The Scarlet, half drunk already, listening to every word.

Dave was the only one who didn't care about things like that. His face had been growing redder and redder ever since Christie read out Mae's note, and he suddenly spoke, very loudly, with no introduction.

'It's not *your* band, Christie.'

Cheers from The Scarlet. I think they expected a good punch-up to follow. A floor show to entertain them while they were waiting to do their next set. But none of us said a word. Dave and Christie glared as they stood obstinately facing each other and then—amazement!—*Christie* stamped out of the room, without an explanation. He spent the rest of that break walking up and down the pavement outside in the cold night air.

When we finished our last set, Mae was standing waiting for us at the top of the spiral staircase, blocking out the light.

'Well? Made up your minds?'

Christie stood at the bottom with his head tilted right back, looking at her. 'We want total artistic control.'

'Poop!' Her laugh was like a slap in the face. 'If you have total artistic control you'll cut your own throats within six months. Seen it happen a million times. You can have *reasonable* artistic control.'

Christie put a foot on the staircase. 'We want to stick with Job's songs. None of anyone else's rubbish.'

'O.K.' Mae nodded. 'The arrangements stink, but the songs are fine. I can live with that.'

Christie went up another step. 'No messing about with our image. We'll hear what you've got to say about our arrangements, but we're not being tarted up to suit your idea of what a band ought to be.'

'For Heavens sake!' Mae said. 'I'm not an idiot. When you're my size and shape you don't buy anything that comes along and try and alter it to fit you. You have to choose the right thing in the first place. I *like* Kelp. But I liked it most when it was most itself—in that first song. Right?'

Christie went up the rest of the stairs and we all went with him, until we were crowded together in the narrow corridor at the top. Then, finally, he nodded. 'Right. We'll talk. When and where?'

'Eleven o'clock tomorrow morning. The London office.' Mae slapped her business card into his hand and then rolled off towards Polo's office without waiting for a reply. That's her style. Wham! Pow! and away before you can peel yourself off the floor. But she turned to look at us again as she opened the door. At me, in particular.

'Oh—make sure you write to your mother before you come, Janis. I always deliver on my promises.'

The others fixed on that as a lifebelt. Driving home we

were into heavy discussions about Mae and her character and our chances and whenever they looked like sinking us someone flung in Janis's letter to haul us out again.

'... better borrow my fountain-pen, Finch, so she doesn't smack your bottom for untidy writing....'

'... get Job to make up a few heart-rending sentences for you....'

'... want me to check your spelling?' (That was Dave, and it raised jeers from the others.)

Oh ha. Ha ha. They could treat it all as a great joke, but I knew what Mae meant, all right. That last look of hers had spelt it out. Himmler must have spilled the tale about the money and she wanted that off her back if she was going to take us on. So the letter was serious, all right. No letter, no deal.

Only Christie had picked that up. As they dumped me off at Ida's he leaned backwards and said over his shoulder, 'Post it before we pick you up tomorrow.'

'Haven't got any paper, have I?' I said, just for the sake of looking independent. I bounced out of the van, leaving that as my exit line, but I couldn't manage to get my key into the door before Christie stuck his head out of the window and yelled the last word, over the noise of acceleration.

'Ask my mum for some. Seeing you're such mates.'

I grabbed a handful of earth from the narrow, cat-ridden border and chucked it after him, but I was too late and it rattled against the back of the van. The tail-lights vanished round the corner as I opened the door.

At least it seemed as though I'd escaped Ida. The whole place was dark, without even the sound of the T.V. If I *had* to write that letter, I might as well take the chance of hunting out a piece of paper and an envelope without being fussed over. Pushing open the sitting-room door, I flicked the light switch.

No light. But the curtains were open and the glow of the street-lamp outside lit up a figure in a chair, staring at a blank television. For a second I got the real cold shudders. It was too like one of those films where you touch the body and it keels over with a knife in its back.

'Mrs Joyce?'

Very slowly, she looked round. 'Oh,' she said vaguely, 'hallo, Janis. The meter.' Then she turned back to the dead screen.

She's flipped, I thought. *She's really flipped and I'm stuck with picking up the pieces.* I hadn't got any technicolour ideas about raving maniacs, mind. I knew what was going on. Ida was like Mum before Himmler, only worse. Way, way down, so low she was shivering in the dark. She couldn't even be bothered to get up and shove a couple of coins in a slot.

The simplest thing was to go on up to bed and leave her. She was hardly going to freeze to death before morning and why should I get mixed up with her? I'd already done my share with Mum. Ida could stew.

But the words seemed to come out by themselves. 'Where's my cup of cocoa?'

'What?' She blinked and looked round, properly this time.

'My *cocoa*. I thought you were going to make me a cup of cocoa at bedtime.'

'Oh—' Her face screwed up with the effort of just thinking about getting out of the chair.

'Come on. I'll come into the kitchen and talk to you while you make it.' I hauled her to her feet and pushed her ahead of me. By the time I'd fed the meter with one of my precious fifty pences and she had got the milk out of the fridge, she looked a bit less like a zombie and I remembered that I needed to get her to find me some paper. Better not hassle her, though. Best to let her make the cocoa first. So I watched the filthy stuff coming to the boil, like diluted sludge, and washed us up a couple of mugs. There's a lot of fussing goes into making a proper cup of cocoa and it livened her up nicely.

Then we got to the tough bit. Drinking it. I took a token sip and murmured, 'Oh, by the way, I've got to write to my mum tonight. You wouldn't have some paper and an envelope, would you?'

She shuffled out of the room and I took a quick leap across to the sink, tipped the cocoa down and ran the tap to destroy the evidence. By the time Ida came back, I was sitting at the table doing a good imitation of someone full of cocoa. A neat operation. Ida looked pretty spritely, too, and I reckoned it would be O.K. to grab the paper and go off to wrestle with my letter.

But she didn't hand it over at once. She stood with it in her hand, looking spaniel-eyed at me. 'I suppose you'll be telling your mother about the band and everything.'

Fat chance. As if I was going to pour it all into Himmler's ever-eager ears. Still, I nodded, to save trouble.

Ida sighed. 'Chris never tells me anything. I don't even know if it's going well or not.'

And there she was, looking at me, with the paper and envelopes clutched in her hand, like a little kid eyeing the biggest cake on the plate. *Oh Finch, you stupid crone, split. Get up to your room, now, before she wheedles a bedtime story out of you.*

Leaning back in my chair, I put my feet up on the table and reached for a biscuit. 'Something happened tonight, as a matter of fact. Could be a fantastic break, but we can't tell yet. And you know what Christie's like. Everything for the band has to be perfect.'

Ida smiled, sentimentally. 'Just like the North Star.'

'I *beg* your pardon?' I crunched the custard cream and stared at her.

'I can see them up in that back bedroom now.' She wasn't really answering me. Just rambling on to herself. 'George putting it together, talking about how every little part had to be just so, and Christie sitting there, with his chin in his hands, drinking it all in.'

'The *North Star?* What on earth are you talking about?'

She blinked at me. 'Christopher . . . his dad. . . .' Then she looked down at her hands, sounding bewildered. 'It was a long time ago, Janis. A terrible long time ago.'

Sure was. When Christie was a (dear?) little boy and that chilly dusty house had a family in it, instead of just Ida, drooping in front of the T.V. For some reason, I wanted to thump the table and yell, not at poor old Ida, but at Things and the way they turned out.

Then she looked up at me again and smiled a small, nervous smile. 'So what was it? That happened tonight?'

It was broad daylight before I got away and I felt like collapsing. Ida didn't nag or ask for more, mind. Just sat there, big-eyed, listening to everything, and smiling when I mentioned Christie's name. It was pathetic. I put in most of the details, just to give her her money's worth, and by the end she was quite lively, giggling at my imitations of Mae and Polo and clapping when I sang her a bit of 'Save Your Breath'. I cut out the hassle about Himmler, of course, because he was none of her business. What I told her was the cleaned-up, fairy-tale version.

But I didn't forget the real one. When I finally crawled up to my room, I had the paper in my hand and I made myself sit down straight away and write the letter. Just put the date, of course, and no address, because there was no point in stirring up trouble.

Dear Mum,

I am well and I hope you are too. I've been working hard and things seem to be going O.K. I am staying with someone's mother and the room's not a palace, but it's bearable.

Love,

Janis

(after only a couple of weeks of being Finch, that was already strange to write. And, as I wrote it, I wondered if, perhaps, it would be the last time. Perhaps, soon, no one would know that there was Janis Mary, hiding behind the Finch disguise)

P.S. Sorry about the money. I will pay it back as soon as I can.

It still looked short, even with the P.S., but there didn't seem to be anything else I could tell her, so I slapped it into the envelope, licked the flap and scrawled the address on the front. Right, that was it, I thought, as I crawled into bed to try and grab an hour or so of sleep. I'd done what Mae wanted and now we'd see what she came up with.

It took me a long time to go to sleep, though.

Chapter 9

When I came round again, I was groggy and tired, with my mind floating somewhere near the ceiling, not quite in contact with reality. Which was a pity, because that first business meeting with Mae was one of the most important mornings of my life. Christie may have landed me with being Finch, but it was Mae who wanted Finch/Janis/me up front for the whole world to stare at. She made that perfectly clear from the beginning.

No hustle, mind. Before she ever said a word, she left us time to be impressed by her office and, although we'd meant to be subzero cool, it impressed us all right.

As her secretary opened the door, the room stretched ahead of us, not wide but almost thirty foot long. For the first two thirds, it was narrowed almost to a corridor by cupboards. They covered the windowless walls on either side, hiding reference books, files and colour samples, telephones, computer terminals and drawing-board behind their storm-grey smoked-glass doors. Beyond them, like a magic island floating in a wintry sea, the room opened out across its full width into silver and pale green, carpeted and upholstered and full of light. And there was Mae, like a Dragon Queen, watching us from the depths of a huge silver armchair. We walked the length of the room, trying to look casual and wondering who the little guy beside her was—grey and shrivelled, with bright, bright eyes. She left us time to sit down and take him in, too, before she introduced him.

'Stanley Grierson. My husband and business partner.'

Nobody said a word while Mae poured us all coffee—from an art nouveau coffee-pot of silver and pale green enamel with a naked girl for a handle. The cups were translucent pale green lustre and the silver sugar-tongs were shaped like a slender, elegant alligator, every line on his skin perfectly marked. We all got the message: *I don't need you like you need me, I'm doing nicely already.* Rollo goggled like a six-year-old visiting the Crown Jewels, and Dave scowled in a pathetic attempt to look unaffected. But we all left the talking to Christie.

'Well?' He balanced his coffee spoon on one finger. 'Come on, persuade us. What are you offering?'

Stanley choked slightly into his coffee, as if he couldn't believe we would dare to bargain, but Mae had a good salesman's poker-face. And too much sense to answer the question directly. Instead, she waited until we were all listening and then began to talk softly, looking into her cup.

'It's hard to handle something really different, really new. If you launch it too soon, people don't know what you're talking about. If you leave it too long, it's dead. You need a special kind of nose for the *moment,* for how people are feeling and thinking. And I've got that. London's full of little Mae Griersons, all doing what I did *last* year, but none of them will ever catch up with me, because they're only copyists.'

'And now you've smelt *us* out?' Job raised an eyebrow. 'Who are you complimenting—us or yourself?'

'You—when you sang that first song.' Mae was crisper now. Business-like. 'If that's the way you want to develop, Stanley and I are prepared to invest money in the band. If not, get out and stop wasting my time. You may make a living, but you'll never be anywhere near my league.'

Beside me, Dave was starting to steam, his face growing red. At any moment, he was likely to come out with one of his moronic, twelve-year-old's insults. Just in time, I stepped on his toe, hard, and while he caught his breath Rollo spoke into the gap.

'But music isn't really your patch, is it? Have you got any other groups at all? And if not, why are you so keen to take us over when it's bound to be a risk?'

Mae grinned. 'How about money? Anyone can do with

another million or so.' Then, more seriously, 'But it's not only that. It's because I saw what you could be, I knew what the band could achieve, if it was handled properly—and I want to test it out. The biggest high of all is *being proved right*. Like God, controlling the stars.'

'Hyper,' said Job, who never misses a pun. 'And you're sticking your neck out that far on the basis of one song? With an inexperienced singer?'

'Oh, I know that's the biggest hazard,' Mae said. 'But it's her I want. Without her, you're about as exciting as a day-trip to Woolworth's.'

Suddenly everyone was looking at me, with their thoughts so plain I could have drawn in the speech bubbles myself. *She's only a kid. Can she take the pressure?* It was obvious they were waiting for a gesture. Janis Mary would have given a big smile and said how much she was looking forward to being a mega-star, with Auntie Mae and Uncle Stanley to hold her hand, but I could see they wouldn't be happy with that. It was Finch they wanted.

I put my feet up on the table—boots and all—in among the porcelain coffee-cups. Folding my arms, I said, 'Why don't we quit horsing about? We all want to do business. The question is, what are you going to give us to make it worth our while? And what are you going to screw out of us in return?'

Click. Even with half an eye on her precious coffee-cups, Mae relaxed visibly. I debated whether to spit into the sugar-basin, but I decided that would be over the top. Rollo would be sure to spoil everything by looking shocked.

'I like straight talk,' Mae said, 'and I'll give you straight answers. When you've done this recording on Thursday—'

'No.'

She blinked. It was the first time Christie had caught her on the hop. 'No what? I haven't suggested anything yet.'

'Yes you have.' Christie was very cool. Even though we had agreed to let him handle things, I could see the others wondering what he was up to. 'We can't start recording on Thursday, because the band you're signing doesn't exist yet. Oh, we found the right set-up last night, and we agree that we want to go that way, but it needs hours of rehearsal before we can produce that sound all the time. So—pay us a salary for four weeks, to give us the chance to forget about drumming up gigs, and we'll work flat out. You can tell Philip Tissiman to come back in a month.'

I almost ducked, waiting for Mae to explode. Why should she keep us on our backsides for a month and send Philip Tissiman packing like a cub come bob-a-jobbing? Dave was grinning all over his stupid face, because he likes a fight, but I could tell from Job's narrowed eyes that he was thinking, like me, that Christie had blown everything.

'A fortnight,' Mae said. Quite calmly.

Christie grinned. 'Three weeks.'

'Done. Now let's get down to details. Stanley. . . .'

We deserved to get ripped off, going in there like that with no lawyer of our own and no proper idea of what we were going to ask. But Stanley was fair. We didn't get jam on it, but we got a reasonable slice of everything. Mae had enough sense to see that we needed an incentive to carry us through the hard work of the next three weeks.

And it *was* hard work. We rehearsed almost all the time, with only a couple of gigs to interrupt us. By rights, we should have finished up shattered, clawing at each other's throats, but in fact it was magic. Perhaps the best time the band's ever had.

I don't know that I could have spelt out the change for you, but it had something to do with my part in everything. Instead of tracking along just behind Christie, I was out on my own as lead singer, with Christie free to improvise or double or sing harmonies. And instead of niggling on at me about particular notes or phrases, he let me relax into the songs, using them to tease him, to snarl back at him, to sulk at him. Everything started to slide into place and the real style of the band began to come through. The true, tough, ironic Kelp sound. There's nothing to match a discovery like that and we spent those three weeks on a continuous rising high, working up towards the recording session. By the time we drove off to Joe Busby's, we thought we had everything at our fingertips and we were impatient to get it down on tape. The rest of the world, outside the band and 'Save Your Breath', might have stopped existing.

Which is why the shock when we got there was like a slap in the face. We thought Mae had understood us, but when we went into the studio building she came to meet us with a glass of champagne in one hand and a silly grin on her face.

'All set? Great. I've asked a few people along to hear the session. To create a bit of interest in the band.'

'You *what?*' It was her turn to startle Christie and I felt him go tense with anger.

'Oh, don't worry.' Incredibly, Mae patted him on the head. Then she ruffled *my* hair, just for good measure. 'They won't disturb you. They're all in the control room. You go on into the studio there and set up and I'll send Philip Tissiman out to you in a minute.'

She sailed off, like an airship, and Job gave one of his weird, sour chuckles. 'So it's a performance, is it? Think they're expecting a full stage show, or will they just clap every track as we lay it down? She's insane.' He pushed open the studio door and glanced towards the big glass panel that separated the studio from the control room. Another chuckle. 'Ever felt sorry for the monkeys at the zoo?'

It was exactly like being on show in a cage. The control room was crammed far too full for anyone to work in there. A dozen people at least were chattering away behind the glass, pointing at us as we carried our gear in. They were all guzzling champagne, but no one looked like offering us any.

'Cream!' said Dave sulkily. He was carrying the suitcase that held the electric piano and he dumped it down, too roughly. 'What does she expect us to do now?'

'You heard what she said,' purred Job. 'Don't know *how* she expects us to set up, mind, before we've had a chance to discuss anything with Philip Tissiman. We'd just be wasting our time.'

'But what *can* we do?' Rollo said miserably. 'How do they think they're going to hear anything good from us with everyone crashing round in there and staring at us?'

'I hate to disillusion you, sunshine,' said Job, busy unpacking the piano. 'That lot in there haven't come to listen to us. They've just come for a party, to humour Mae. Oh, I guess someone'll come out in an hour or so and they'll knock up some kind of recording, but I wouldn't raise your hopes too high if I were you.' He plugged in the leads. 'Funny, though, because she seemed quite serious before. Can't imagine what she's up to.' He began to play, with the headphones on, cutting himself off from the rest of us.

'Well, I think we should complain!' Dave said fiercely.

'Yes,' said Christie.

He had been utterly still and quiet while the rest of us raged and even now his voice was quite quiet. He stopped for a second, looking at me like a cat stalking a bird and then he nodded.

'You go Finch.'

'Me?' I stared at him. 'You've got to be crazy.'

But then they were all looking at me, except Job, and the only way out was to simper and squeal, *Not me, I can't do something like that.* No way out for me. I shrugged and walked out into the corridor, banging the door after me.

The control room was only a few strides along the corridor. A couple of seconds to make up my mind what I was going to do. I guessed that Christie or Job would have made a cold, angry complaint, very cutting and dignified, but I wasn't Christie or Job. I was me and I was furious and I wanted a way to let the fury out. How *dared* they get us there to patronize us and make fun of us? What made Mae think she could get away with it? Just bursting in and yelling at them all wasn't good enough. I needed a siren to deafen them, a hammer to break that huge glass window, a cat to throw into the middle of the room with its claws scrabbling.

And then I saw the crate of champagne outside the control room door and my hands reached for the nearest bottle, picked it up and shook it thoughtfully a few times. Slowly, my fingers began to peel off the foil top.

Of course, I wasn't going to do anything. Everyone has a thousand weird ideas every day that never go beyond a quick flicker in the mind. But then, on the other side of the door, a man laughed. Nothing special, just a short, superior, *adult* laugh, but I could imagine the man who'd made it. The band would be kids to him, people to be pushed around and allowed to make money for him but left out of the serious discussions. The way Himmler had cut me out with Mum. I looked down at the bottle in my hands and thought, *Finch*.

Holding my breath, I unwound the wire from the cork, shook the bottle again, hard, and kicked the door open as I pushed the cork off with my thumbs. I think I shouted aloud—'Kiai!'—the way Bernard had taught me to yell when I was launching a blow, because heads turned as I pointed the bottle into the room and let it spurt, spraying it wildly, machine-gunning champagne on to expensive hair and silk shirts, into open mouths and goggle eyes. And all the time I was screaming words that were almost nonsense, they were so full of anger.

'Want to suck our blood, do you? Keep us on a string? Make chimpanzees of us? *We're* the strong ones! *We're* the real ones! You're just cardboard people! Leeches! Parasites!'

Or something like that. How can I remember exactly? I was way, way up in the clouds, too far gone to think what I looked like or what I was doing to the band's chances. All I knew was that for once, for a split second or so, I had the upper hand of the string-pullers.

It was only a second or two. Then someone laid a hand on my arm and I dropped the bottle, letting it smash on the ground, and stood staring at them. Nothing shows people up like having their hair drenched. The balding ones and the wrinkled ones were suddenly dripping and pathetic. The old-young ones, who had been straining their faces to look alert and sexy, were shocked into showing what they really were—pompous and annoyed and middle-aged. For perhaps ten seconds, with the adrenalin whizzing round me, I felt fantastic, and then the picture in front of me turned inside out and I thought. *I've ruined everything.*

As I thought it, I glanced at Mae, expecting—oh, I don't know—rage? Disappointment? After all, I'd loused up her carefully-prepared show. *She was smiling.* Almost as I saw it, she rearranged her face and was coming forward, looking wry and apologetic.

'Well—' a small shrug, with her hands spread '—you can see I wasn't boasting. This is Finch.'

Someone said bitterly, 'I hope she can sing as well as she shoots champagne.'

'Fancy demonstrating?' Mae raised an eyebrow at me. She must be insane.

'We're not poodles,' I said. 'We came to make a recording. Get this lot out of here or we're going straight home.'

There's nothing like quitting on a good line. I banged out of the room before anyone could get in with a come-back and almost ran down the corridor and into the studio. The boys were falling about, totally ignoring the fact that everyone could see them.

'Cream!' said Dave as I came through the door. 'Double cream. Hyper hyper. Did you see that fat guy in the yellow linen jacket?' He creased up.

'We shouldn't be laughing,' Rollo said. 'They can't help being—being—' But he was choking on the words as he said them and even Job was smiling. Even Christie.

'What's so whoopee?' I kept in the doorway, out of view of the control room. I wasn't making my second thoughts public. 'Can't you dodos see I've blown it? Sky-high. To kingdom come. Those were Mae's star contacts, and they weren't exactly purring.'

'You cloth-head, Finch!' Christie said. 'You pea-brain!'

I would have forced him to explain, but at that moment a tall, nervous-looking man appeared in the doorway. A bit damp, but perfectly cheerful.

'Philip Tissiman.' He nodded at us all and looked warily at me. 'I think we should get down to it, don't you?'

I was still hyped up when I got home at two o'clock in the morning, my whole body buzzing with the excitement of that session. The others just dumped me off, as usual. It was obvious that they were going back to the flat to sit and talk and drink coffee. After a really good recording session, you need time to work yourself down from the cloud you're perched on. But Christie tipped me out of the van as if it had been any other night and left me stranded on the pavement, with no one to unload to. So I knocked up Ida.

I did it the decent way, with a mug of cocoa and a plate of biscuits. She always swore she never closed her eyes *all night,* but there was plenty of snoring going on when I kicked the door open and switched on the light.

'It's your lucky evening, Mrs Joyce! Refreshments *and* a cabaret!'

'What?' She woke all at once, sitting bolt upright and cowering back against the wall, like someone leaping out of a nightmare.

'Cocoa?' I held it out to her. 'Custard cream?'

'Janis, what's the matter?' But she took them, sipped the boiling mud and nibbled the biscuit. I sat on the end of the bed.

'We've made the greatest recording in the world! We've sung and played a million times better than ever before!'

She clued in straight away, cuddling her knees up underneath her night-dress and settling herself ready to listen. Even though I went on for an hour and a half, before I calmed down enough to go to bed, she never yawned once.

Dear Mary Dashwood

I have recently remarried, but my sixteen-year-old daughter never got on with my new husband and two months ago she ran away to London. Since then, I've only had one letter and that had no address on it, so there's no way I can get in touch with her.

I have been desperately worried about her, but she's always been tough and independent and it sounds as though she has somewhere reasonable to stay, so I was going to let her work things out for herself. However, I have just learnt that I have cancer. My husband says he will go to London and track her down so that he can have her brought home. I know we would be within our legal rights, but I'm sure that would be the end of everything. My daughter would never forgive me. On the other hand, how will she feel if she doesn't come back until it's too late? Please tell me what you think I should do.

You have my greatest sympathy in this difficult time. I definitely think you should try to find out where your daughter is, if that's possible. Just because she's run away it doesn't mean that she doesn't love you. But, if you do manage to track her down, instead of forcing her back, why not write her a letter, telling her the situation? In that way, you leave the choice open to her without invading her privacy and, if she cares about you, I'm sure she will respond.

Chapter 10

Next morning it was tit for tat, only without the cocoa and biscuits. I was somewhere way down deep when a small squeaking began in my ear and nervous fingers prodded at me, dragging me out from under twenty tons of sleep.

'Janis. Telephone.'

I opened my eyes and saw a sight that would have sent anyone diving back under the covers. Ida, in a dear little Donald Duck pinny, waving a feather duster. I shut my eyes again.

'*Janis!* It's that Mae Grierson.'

'No,' I said. Meaning, *Go away until tomorrow*. But at the same time, my legs were kicking their way out from under the covers and my arms were finding a jumper to drag on. 'What time is it?'

'Eleven o'clock. Janis you've got to—'

'O.K. O.K.' I groaned and tottered downstairs to the phone. 'Finch.'

'Mae.' No time wasted on politeness. 'I want the whole band down at my office at four o'clock.'

I looked at my white, dead face in the hall mirror. Why not? Robots can do anything. 'What for?'

'Got someone I want you to meet. Could be good. It's Terry Donovan.'

'Who?'

'Ask Christie.' She sounded amused. 'See you at four o'clock. Don't be late.'

End of conversation. Before I had recovered enough to put the phone down, Ida was calling me from upstairs.

'Is everything all right?'

That's the trouble with talking to people like her. Tell

them one thing and they expect to be let in on all your secrets for ever. I grunted and bumbled my way up the stairs, intending to sneak back into my room without getting trapped into a chat.

But there was something blocking my way at the top of the stairs. Sleepy and stupid, I stared at it for a good ten seconds before I realized that it was the door of the back bedroom. It was hung the other way round, so that it opened out on to the landing and, for the first time since I had been there, it was open when I could see it.

'In here!' Ida called.

I winkled my way round the door—only to find something else blocking off the door space. A sort of shelf, with rails on, ran across it at waist height. *Rails?*

Ida waved her feather duster at me from the other side. 'You have to duck under.'

'Athletic,' I said, ducking.

It was a lunatic's room. The shelf ran all the way round the walls and crossed the middle of the room a couple of times so that the whole place was divided up into tiny sections. And on the far side, where the shelf was wide enough to carry a station, stood the North Star.

You can just wipe out whatever picture you've got in your head so far, because, unless you're a model railway freak, you'll never have seen an engine like the North Star. It was somewhere around a foot long and almost as high, if you counted the tall, narrow funnel. And every spoke in the wheels, every strip of brass and rivet head was fanatically, neurotically perfect. Ducking under another piece of rail, I went to take a close look at it.

'Isn't it beautiful?' Ida said in the kind of soggy voice that makes you want to have your ears amputated. 'George always liked the broad gauge best. Brunel was his hero.'

'*Who?*' I said, not taking my eyes off the crazy engine.

'Brunel.' Ida flapped her hand towards a photograph on the wall. A stocky guy in a top hat, standing in front of enormous chains. I looked at him for a moment, wondering if he was Christie's hero too. Then I turned back to that amazing, detailed, precise engine. *So it's your fault is it, George?* I thought. He was the person the rest of the band should blame for all the hours and hours of flogging away at one line. The man who had taught Christie to niggle on and on in search of perfection. I reached out to pick up the North Star, feeling its weight and running my finger up the curve of the funnel. There was a yelp from behind me that nearly made me drop it. I looked round. 'What's up?'

Ida had gone a pale pea-green and she was holding on to the narrow table-top in front of her. 'Please,' she whispered. 'Please put it down.'

'Why?' I grinned at her and turned the engine sideways. 'I'm not hurting it.'

'But if you drop it—Chris'll *kill* me if anything happens to that locomotive.'

She was dead serious. Oh, I know people say things like that all the time. Mum used to do it. *Dad'll kill me if tea's not ready by six.* Family Games. (Not with Himmler, though. Too busy playing Great Lovers.) But Ida wasn't making any kind of joke. She looked ready to pass out.

'It's only a toy,' I said.

'Of course it's not!' She bristled, the way you do when someone gets your family's speciality wrong. 'It's a scale model—and I don't know what Chris will do if you damage it. *Please,* Janis.'

'O.K. O.K.' I put it down on the rails and walked back across the room. 'Haven't got time to fiddle around with it anyway. Got to go out.'

Then I ducked through the door, meanly, and made off before she could ask me where I was going.

'Mae said *what?*' Christie yelped when I strolled into the flat with my news. 'What's going on?'

'Don't know.' I pulled the blankets off Dave, who was still snoring, and went to put the kettle on. It didn't seem a good moment to tease Christie about toy trains. 'She didn't tell me anything else.'

'What have you got for brains? Bread sauce?' Christie followed me into the back room. 'Why didn't you *ask?*'

'Oh sure.' I held out a match to the gas ring and then jumped back to avoid getting my eyebrows blown off. 'I just adore asking dumb questions. If she'd wanted us to know, she would have told us, wouldn't she? Anyway, what are you getting steamed up about?'

'Steamed up?' Christie rolled his eyes up at the ceiling and Job hooted with laughter in the other room. 'When did they dig you out of the pyramids? Terry Donovan's *only* the A & R man for Zombie, that's all. Every band you've ever met would swim through boiling porridge to meet him.'

Rollo looked round the door, yawning so wide I nearly fell into his mouth. 'It's success, folks! He's heard our demo tape and he's desperate to sign us. He'll offer us anything!'

'That's right!' Dave blundered in and wandered round the kitchen in his underpants, looking for something to eat. 'He's fallen in love with my photograph and he's dying to plaster it all over a record sleeve so the whole *world* can fall in love with me. We'll be millionaires!'

'Get out the Littlewoods catalogue,' called Job. 'I want to order three Porsches and a gold-plated lavatory seat.'

'Terry Donovan, Terry beautiful, beautiful Donovan!' trilled Dave, smearing peanut butter on to the end of a stale loaf. 'Clap your hands if you believe in magic!'

Job and Rollo clapped dementedly, while Dave rambled on, cramming bread and peanut butter into his mouth like a JCB trying to fill in a quarry. But Christie was as sour as last week's milk. You could see it in his expression—he wanted to plan this meeting and get us all organized for it, but he couldn't because he hadn't got enough information. Like trying to play trains without the points. Oh, he and that super-perfect train set were made for each other. I turned my back and started digging a spoon into the coffee jar. *You'll just have to lump it, Christie Joyce. Go into this meeting like a human being, instead of acting the Great Controller in the sky.*

The Dragon Queen had a Gorilla on her magic island when the secretary showed us in that afternoon. At the far end of the long, dark corridor of cupboards, Mae sat regal and silent, listening to a loud monologue from the hairiest man I've ever seen. Oh, nothing corny like the open shirt and the gold medallion round his neck. He was wearing an ordinary T-shirt and a pair of jeans. But pretty well every visible bit of him was sprouting black curls, and the hair on his head and his chin were cropped to about an inch, so that he looked furry all over. While he talked, he rubbed at his cheek or his forearm or his head, like a gorilla chasing fleas.

Christie coughed from the doorway.

The Gorilla didn't even draw breath. Rattled on with his monkey chatter. '. . . that's fifty per cent up. *Fifty per cent,* Mae. Do you realize . . . ?

Mae gave us a sideways look, as comprehensible as a rubber tin-opener, and then turned back to the jungle noises. Jerking his head, Christie set us walking, slow and noisy, down between the cupboards. When we came into the light, we spread out, taking all the empty seats, but still no one spoke to us. Hardly taking her eyes off the Gorilla, Mae poured us all diddy cups of tea and handed round the cream buns. The Gorilla took one without even looking and kept it in his hand as he talked. The bun never quite made it to his mouth. Each time it sneaked near, he would start another sentence and whisk it away again in a great, swirling gesture.

'. . . got to be aware of the problems of being under-capitalized. . . .'

Unbelievable! He was boasting about Zombie's success. That was like racing into the room and saying, *I've just been to Paris and there's this fantastic tower designed by someone called Eiffel!* Even toddlers knew that Zombie was the biggest thing since Jack's Beanstalk. We wanted news. *We* wanted to talk about Kelp.

Fifteen minutes later, we were still waiting. Hadn't even

been introduced. I saw Christie kick Mae's ankle once or twice, but that had no more effect than kicking the British Museum. It seemed like she was ignoring us on purpose, struggling not to look at us—but that was ridiculous.

Then I began to feel the eyes. Job first. Don't know when it started, but I suddenly realized he was watching me from under careful eyelids as I sat there fuming. No expression on his face, of course.

Rollo was the next one to pick it up, but there's nothing deadpan about him. WORRY was stencilled all over his forehead. Every time I tapped my toe or sighed, he gave a nervous twitch, until I began to feel like an unexploded bomb.

And still the Gorilla was grunting out statistics.

After a while, my skin got to itch. I couldn't find a comfortable way to hold my hands and I kept catching sight of the end of my nose. I wanted to kick the table over, throw the tiny porcelain teacups on the floor, empty the teapot into Terry Donovan's lap. But for another five minutes I managed to keep more or less still.

Then Christie looked at me. Up till then, he'd been glaring down at his feet, but suddenly he lifted his head as if he'd just cottoned on to something and I saw his face relax. He stared straight at me, like that first time in the café, daring me. Rollo caught his breath and Job gave a slow, lopsided grin.

Why me? Why *me?*

Ever watched a pressure-cooker? It looks peaceful enough from outside, but all the time the steam's building up and if it weren't for the valve it would splatter itself all over the ceiling. That valve just has to blow to let off steam.

All the band was looking at me now, and Mae *wasn't* looking, as hard as she could. And the Gorilla was still grunting on, waving his bun about. And Christie was still taunting me with his eyes. And the band and Mae and the Gorilla and Christie and thebandandMaeandtheGorillaand-thebun and Christie . . . and Christie . . . and Christie. . . .

'*Yawn!*' I said, very loud, right in the middle of a sentence.

The Gorilla stopped and looked at me for the first time. Very blue eyes he had, not half as dumb as I'd expected. But I was launched now.

'Why don't you give that cream bun a *chance?*' I said, sweet as an air hostess. 'Here, I'll help you.'

I grabbed up the last bun from the plate, stared him straight in the eye and squashed it into his open mouth. The cream squelched over my fingers and smeared his face like snow on a fur coat, but the blue eyes stayed steady.

'Finch!' Whatever Mae was expecting, I'd topped her wildest dreams. Catapulted us into Cartoon Time with a custard pie in the face of our Big Break. But if she thought I was going to apologize, she was raving. I stood up.

'Stuff your sacred recording company,' I said, slowly and clearly. 'How desperate do you think we are? If you wanted to sign us, you should have treated us like people. We're not a tame band.'

Then I left, fast, before the horror could hit me. Somewhere behind me, I heard a splutter and a giant laugh, and as I reached the door someone called 'Finch!' but I wasn't going back. I caught a bus to Buckingham Palace and walked up and down the Mall until it was dark, with policemen eyeing me nervously.

'You *must* have realized it was a set-up!' Christie said. 'With Mae sitting there all wound up in case we let her down and behaved like angels.'

It was around ten o'clock when I staggered home. Ida tweeted at me from the front room and when I put my head round the door there they all were, the whole band, guzzling cocoa while Ida beamed like it was her birthday.

When they'd gabbled on at me all together for a couple of minutes, I flopped on to the floor, none the wiser, trying to ignore the cup of cocoa waving around under my nose. Job put a hand on my head.

'Quiet, you lot, before Finch goes volcanic. It's Uncle

Job's storytime. Are you sitting comfortably, Finch?'

'Great. Fantastic,' I said. 'The floor's like a feather bed. Why don't you get *on* with it?' There's nothing I hate worse than being the only person in the room who doesn't know what's going on. It was obvious from Christie's smug face that there was some kind of joke on me.

Job tweaked my ear gently. 'Once upon a time, there was a hairy A & R man who went to see his fairy godmother. "Please, fairy godmother," he said, "I need a new, exciting band." So—fizzz!—his fairy godmother waved her magic wand and played him a sensational demo tape of a band who—'

'Do I *have* to listen to all this?' I said.

I might just as well have saved my breath. Job ignored the interruption and went on in the same singsong chant, '—sounded like his wildest day-dreams. His fairy godmother told him they were ee-lectric. Independent and full of aggro—especially the lead singer who'd sprayed champagne over Al Charlton from Clogs. But the A & R man thought he was too old for magic. He'd been had before by bands who pretended to be independent but who were ready to lick the boots of anyone from a recording company.'

'Ah. Poor little A & R man,' said Dave, taking another handful of custard creams.

'So he set up a test, taking good care that the fairy godmother couldn't warn the band. *And*—'

As Job paused dramatically, Rollo burst in. 'And you were fantastic, Finch! Double cream. *Clotted* cream!'

'Clotted nonsense,' I said, picking the skin off my cocoa and swallowing hard to try and get rid of the lump in my throat. I'd been tricked. Made a fool of. *And Christie had guessed what was going on.* Remembering the look he had given me, I was sure of it, and I gathered my breath, searching for the words to bawl him out.

But before I could say anything, he smiled, a slow smile that spread across his face like one of those films of a flower opening. 'It was great, Finch. Couldn't have been better. Here. Thought you deserved a reward.'

I must have had vicarage tea in my veins, because I just

smiled back at him, while my body turned weak and warm. For a second or two, I didn't even glance down to see what he was giving me as a reward for letting myself be manipulated. And when I did, I nearly laughed out loud at the irony of it.

It was the nunchaku, the beautiful, ferocious weapon that Bernard had given him when he was thirteen.

Chapter 11

All good fairy-tale stuff, you see. First our heroes find their fairy godmother (disguised as a Total Environment Specialist) and then they defeat the dragon (disguised as a gorilla) and win a recording contract. The next step, of course, is making a magic single that shoots—whizz! pow!—straight to the top of the charts.

But it wasn't quite like that. Oh, I'm not saying there's anything desperate wrong with 'Streatham Nights'. We were really pleased with it at the time. Christie rehearsed us so hard before the recording that we could have done the song in our sleep and then Philip Tissiman, still pale and polite and chewing his finger-nails, took over with the same niggling, exact determination to be perfect. Every track laid down separately and recorded and re-recorded until the notes seemed like nonsense. When he'd finished playing his games and we listened to the final mix, we hardly recognized it as the song we'd sung with our ordinary human voices. It was a super-spotless electro-song and we all imagined that it would be zapping back at us from every radio in earshot within two months.

The opening is still the noisiest thing we've ever done—drums, keyboards, guitar and harmonica all at once and, over the top, my voice as hard and cold as black ice pouring out one of Job's best tunes with Christie shadowing me:

'I hate to walk the streets alone at night. . . .'

It's strong, without missing out on the music, and it's got one of the most riveting hooks in the business, when the whole lot cuts out suddenly and there's just me singing with Christie gliding underneath, so softly that you're not quite sure your ears aren't playing tricks. Like the footfall you hear behind you in the dark, that you hope you're imagining. And that lovely, toe-curling melody:

> *'And it's not your guardian angel, girl,*
> *That's coming at you through the darkness of the Streatham Nights.'*

Not a bad record, but a dead end. We flogged ourselves to death making it and then it was something else, something we didn't want at all, that turned out to be the real break.

I can still *taste* the moment when I first heard about it. A mixture of liquorice and biro ink. I'd got an advance of a hundred pounds from Mae and I was in my room, eating my way through a quarter of sweets and struggling with the most difficult letter of my life. Searching for careful, tactful words that would wipe out all the trouble between Mum and me and put us back to where we were before I left. Or, better, to where we were before Himmler came.

Suddenly, the whole house rattled. The front door slammed, feet pounded upstairs and, from below, there was an uncontrolled scream of rage.

'You dare—you *dare* treat me like that!'

For a moment I didn't even recognize Ida's voice. It hadn't occurred to me that she had the guts to be so angry. She came galloping upstairs, still yelling, and when I poked my head out of the room there she was, pounding away at the door of the back bedroom.

'Christopher! Unbolt this door! Come out here and apologize!'

I'm not a fan of interfering in other people's family quarrels, but it was beginning to look as though she would hurt herself, bashing away at the door, so I went and pulled her off. It took all my strength to prise her away without damaging her and even when I had her gripped tight to me she was battering her head against my chest, as if it was a wall, and yelling. 'He thinks he can do anything! He thinks he can stamp on my face!'

No point in trying to talk to her until she'd got it out of her system. Mum once broke every cup in the kitchen before she would let me explain why I was late home. Poor Ida must have burnt up more energy in that ten minutes than in all the time I'd known her, but in the end she relaxed and the noise stopped, except for her breath rasping in her throat. Even then I didn't ask questions. There was no need.

'He came racing in like a maniac,' she mumbled. 'Looked terrible. Wouldn't even speak to me. And when I tried to ask—' her voice went shrill, but I gripped her arm until she levelled out again. 'When I tried to ask what the matter was, he pushed me out of the way. Pushed me *over.*'

No exaggeration there. A lump on her cheek-bone was swelling and turning pink. I tried to imagine Christie lashing out like that, but it was impossible. He must have been way out of control and the idea frightened me.

I patted Ida's arm. 'How about making a cup of tea? I'll come down in a minute and I'll try to get Christie to come too. Hey?'

She was so hyped up that, for a second, I thought she was going to argue, but I smiled at her and she trotted off like a lamb. The moment she was gone, I put my ear to the door. No prizes for guessing what Christie was doing. The sound of wheels on rails was unmistakable. I waited for a lull and then tapped on the door.

'Let me in. She's downstairs.'

A pause. Then I heard the bolt slide. When I pulled the door open, Christie was back in the centre of the layout, turning a handle while he watched the North Star moving slowly round a curve.

'Don't jog the track,' he said, before I had a chance to speak.

'Christie—' I ducked under the shelf and into the room.

He didn't look up. 'Mae called us. On the shop phone.'

'Wow.' If there were ten things that drove Mr Liu wild, one was rehearsing out of hours and the other nine were phone calls for the band on the shop line. It must have been really urgent if Mae wasn't bothering with sending messages by me. 'Important?'

'You could say that.' Christie was so angry that his hands were shaking on the controls and even his voice was unsteady. Half of me wanted to back out and leave him to it. Oh sure, I'd seen Christie lose his temper with the band a million times—at least twice every rehearsal—but I'd never seen him come to pieces before.

'Why don't you stop feeling sorry for yourself,' I said, 'and tell me what the big disaster is?'

It took another couple of minutes. We both stood watching the North Star take the curves, with the four carriages clattering after her. Twice round the room and once straight across it on the narrow strip that separated me from Christie. Working perfectly, looking beautiful, utterly under control.

'We're going on tour,' Christie said at last. 'Mae's arranged it all. We start next Tuesday.' The North Star slid into the station. 'We're supporting Nitrogen Cycle.'

Blink. It was a shock, all right. But I couldn't see why it had disintegrated him. I shrugged. 'O.K. So we've got to start touring next Tuesday. It'll be a bit of a rush to get ready, but we can manage. I know it's not great getting stuck with Nitrogen Cycle, but—' Absent-mindedly, I ran my forefinger along the rail nearest me.

'Off!' Christie snapped. 'You'll get grease on the track.' There was no sign of a smile. Leaving the controls, he rubbed at the rail with a cloth.

'Oh come on Christie. You don't have to be so—'

'*A bit of a rush to get ready.*' He spat the words out. 'You don't know what you're talking about. You think we just have to toss a few socks into a suitcase and take our stage act straight out of the Red Lion and into the Liverpool Empire or the Birmingham Odeon? Get professional, Finch. It's a whole different ball game. It would be bad enough being thrown into it like this if we were on a good tour. But—with Nitrogen Cycle? It's got to be death. We're just not in the same business as they are.'

'So why do they want us?'

'They don't want *us.*' His mouth twisted and I heard the North Star begin to move again. 'They're in a hole, that's all, and Mae's used her precious contacts to push us in to plug it. Barry Jackson's cracked up. They carted him off yesterday and that leaves Racing Demon in tatters. *So we're subbing for Racing Demon on the tour.*'

Yes, even I could wince at that. Kelp was no replacement for three cute little madams wiggling their bottoms and smarming round the beautiful Barry Jackson. Singing garbage, just for the sake of putting him up on stage to be swooned over. Even Nitrogen Cycle were more genuine than that.

'We haven't got to *be* them,' I said, stubbornly. 'It's a fantastic chance for us. They may not be our audiences, but they'll be huge ones and by the time we get back people will know about Kelp. And the band needs work. We've done too much sitting around in the last month.'

'Mae's rushing us into things we don't want, without even asking us,' Christie said. 'I knew that was a danger, but I didn't expect it to happen so soon. It's getting out of control. I feel as though I'm losing my grip on the band.'

He was angry, not bidding for sympathy, but for a split second I wanted to duck under the track and grab him. Hold him, hard, until he was together again, the way I had with Ida. I could almost feel his head pressed against my shoulder and his hair tickling my nose. Just one of the sick tricks your mind sometimes plays.

'Diddums!' I said fiercely. 'Going to give in then, are we? Let Auntie Mae run the band for us? Don't be a *slob!* We can knock something good out of this tour if we really try. I know we can.'

I waited just long enough to see his head come up and his back straighten and then I ducked out of the room.

'Tea's ready!' Ida called from downstairs.

'O.K. In a minute.' I was in no state to face anyone yet. The moment I stopped concentrating on Christie, I'd begun to shake. Diving back into my room, I picked up my letter to Mum. Perhaps if I thought hard about that, I'd get back to normal. But my pulse was bumping and my mind felt as though it had been through a food processor. The letter, which had been difficult before I was interrupted, was impossible now.

All along, I'd been thinking that, once I could give the money back, I would be able to apologize properly to Mum, tell her all the news I'd felt too guilty to write before. But how do you begin to tell things to someone who's missed out on the most important months of your life? Every sentence I made up in my mind, however much I meant it, came out and tottered miserably round my bare room like a stranger, looking for the posters and the cushions and the rosy wallpaper that went with Janis Mary. But the only thing hanging on the walls here was my rusty-black ninja suit.

I still had to send the money, though. And, with the tour looming, it was double urgent, because I was likely to be too busy to get another chance. In the end, I shut my mind off, blocking out the noise of the North Star and the thoughts of the tour and scribbled down the first thing that came into my head.

> *Dear Mum,*
>
> *Here's the money I owe you. Sorry it's taken so long to raise. The band I'm with is doing well and we're going on tour soon.*
>
> *Love,*
>
> *Finch*

Folding the paper round the wad of notes, I shoved the lot into the envelope, stuck down the flap and scrawled *Mrs B. Finch* and the address, before I could change my mind. Even if it wasn't perfect, at least it was done.

Chapter 12

And just as well, too, because that was the last free time I had. There were four hectic days to get ready for the tour—hiring extra equipment, trying to book lodgings, rehearsing like mad—and then we were off.

It was three weeks of hell. Three scrambling, sweltering weeks, with Nitrogen Cycle looking down their noses at us and everyone, *everyone,* from tour manager down to the last stage-hand, knowing we were mud. It's bad enough being a support band anyway, trying to perform your best when the kids are mostly itching for you to finish, but being a *substitute* support band is the real scrapings of the sewer.

It was a killing tour anyway, with only three nights off in three weeks and a different town almost every day. We spent most of our time, when we weren't performing, fighting to arrange sound checks. From eight in the morning the stage belonged to the riggers and loaders and electricians and stage-hands and fork-lift operators and the circus in general. It was impossible to do anything, however early we got there.

Once the stage was set up, around four o'clock, Nitrogen Cycle got it for *their* sound check, for as long as they wanted. And it *was* long, believe me. From the fuss they made, you would have thought it was music they were playing, with Nikko stopping neurotically every two minutes to consult with the production manager and Shazz mooning around trying to shake off her hangover.

After that, on any normal tour, we'd have got our turn. But of course Nitrogen Cycle have this gimmick of always including a local band at each gig and the local band got the next bite at the cherry. They were only supposed to take half an hour or so, but of course they always tried to poach more because, being a different band in each place, they always had to start from scratch. Finally, in the end, *if* there was time before the door opened, it was us. We were supposed to check with Nitrogen Cycle's production manager, but after the first day we realized that all he wanted was to keep our equipment off the stage except when we were actually performing, so we short-circuited him.

Some bands tell you all sorts of sob stories about how they've toured as a supporting act and the lead band has hammered them all the time, out of sheer jealousy. We were never in any danger of that. As far as Nitrogen Cycle were concerned, we were about as significant as the tea boy. Oh sure, they had us in for drinks once or twice, so they could play lords of the manor and show what good guys they were, but apart from that we hardly saw them. While we flogged through our set, they were tucked away in the star dressing-room, cocooned in Grade A cotton wool, and by the time they were ready to play we had crawled off to hide.

It may seem all jam and jelly babies, being paid for singing the same thing over and over again, but it's more like climbing a slippery rock-face in plimsolls. You sweat as much the twentieth time as you did the first, and you know a lot more about the dangers. Getting some of those songs right—especially 'Break-out' and 'Streatham Nights'— hyped me up to such a level that I could hardly breathe, hardly see.

But it wasn't succeeding. Night after night, we got polite, tepid applause and we knew we were failing, but it seemed impossible to do anything about it. We didn't have lights or stage design or anything else on our side, because all those were geared to Nitrogen Cycle, and we didn't have our own fans in the audience like the local band. Jed came up a couple of times to trim my hair and stayed on for the evening, but he couldn't make much difference on his own. We were starved of rehearsal time and information and sometimes even food and—

'And we're getting too bloody good at making excuses for ourselves!'

It was Dave, amazingly, who had the guts to say it. At the worst time of all for me, just after we'd finished the Birmingham gig. I was feeling as low as the bottom of a swamp because I'd hoped—stupidly, fantasizing—that Mum would somehow know I was there. Would use the chance to come and see me. While I was busy digesting the fact that she hadn't, Dave was obviously deciding that it was time we faced reality. Loading three spoonfuls of sugar into his coffee, he slopped it on the café table as he stirred it and looked round at us all.

'We can't blame anyone else for the way we're performing. We stink like old socks.'

'Gee, Dave, you are so *fearless*. I do admire you,' drawled Job. But he was sitting up and taking notice, and so was Christie.

'It's true.' Rollo rubbed a hand across his face and pulled unhappily at his hair. 'We've got to talk about it. What are we doing wrong?'

'We're not just *doing* things wrong.' Job put his finger into the puddle of tea that Dave had spilt and drew a perfect triangle. 'We *are* wrong. Us. Kelp.'

He glanced at Christie across the table. Nothing democratic about those two. If they could have sorted things out without consulting the rest of us, they would have been issuing instructions as fast as anyone else on the tour.

Dave did an instant prima donna. 'Oh great. Fantastic. Thanks, Job. We'll junk the whole thing, shall we? Turn in this scabby band and go back on the dole where we belong—'

Job reached out and his long, pale fingers closed over Dave's hand, steadying it. Then I understood. Dave hadn't dragged everything out into the open because he was thick-skinned, but because he was the one who most hated going out in front of an audience and failing. He needed the applause to survive.

'Can it, Dave,' Job said gently. 'I'm not knocking you. Not knocking any of us. The music's O.K., but somehow it's not coming across on-stage. Somehow, we're killing the songs. But I don't know—'

'I do,' Rollo said suddenly. The embarrassment of interrupting made him red-faced, but there was no one to bawl him out. It was so unusual for Rollo to push his own ideas that everyone was curious.

'Well?' Christie said.

'We're killing the music because we're faking,' Rollo said, slowly, like someone working something out as he spoke. 'We've got Finch prancing about doing karate exercises, but she might just as well be wearing a ballet dress and waving a buttercup. It's obviously rehearsed. It just doesn't go with what the songs are about.'

'Which is?' Job said, half amused.

'Danger. Risk,' muttered Rollo. 'Pushing things to the limit and—oh, it sounds dumb to say it, but you know it's true.'

He said it all very nervously, but his words slid into place like hot rivets, pulling everything together. Job's songs *were* dangerous. They never used quite the words you expected or chose the obvious note. They went another three steps and startled you by managing, *just* managing, to be sensationally right, like someone balancing on the very edge of the kerb instead of walking safely along the middle of the pavement.

Only Dave was still adrift. 'What do you want us to do? Bring in machine-guns? Jump into the audience and beat up the kids? Call up the I.R.A. and—'

'Dave,' said Christie.

That stopped him. 'Yeah?'

'Why don't you rest your brain and let the grown-ups work this out?'

It was nothing worse than Christie had said a thousand times before—when you're together all day, every day, you don't make pretty speeches to each other—but that morning, with the record of 'Streatham Nights' plunging like a submarine and our stage show dying as well, it was way, way over the top. Dave's face went beetroot and he jerked forward, pulling his hand away from Job's.

'If you think you can—'

'Yes, Christie,' Job interrupted, smooth as butter, taking over the conversation, 'Dave's not as far out as you think. How do you get *real* danger on to the stage without serious violence? It's all been done before, way beyond anything we can think of. We just haven't got the resources for anything big.'

'We've got ourselves,' Christie said slowly.

'Looks like a spot of self-mutilation, then,' muttered Job.

Christie tapped a finger on the table. 'No. Listen. Rollo didn't say we should be violent. He said we should take risks. What was it you told Terry Donovan, Finch? *We're not a tame band*. That's what we've got to communicate. We've actually got to make something happen. On stage.'

His eyes met mine, with a long, impersonal stare, and I shuddered. 'So what do we do?'

'We work on ourselves,' he said. For another second he stared at me and then, glancing round the table to gather us all together, he began to talk faster, bending his plastic teaspoon in his hands. 'Look, we've had a fairly conventional set so far. Putting in a slow song to let off the tension after something big like 'Break-out'. But I think we should go for that tension, deliberately. Change the order of the songs so that they build up in a solid crescendo, from 'Supernova' right through to 'Streatham Nights'. Let everything get louder and harder and faster, with Finch and me getting closer and closer, until we're yelling into each other's faces. And then—'

'And then?' I said.

The teaspoon snapped in half and Christie smiled, like a kid playing with a chain-saw. 'Then you let it go, Finch. Just be yourself and do whatever comes over you.'

So we changed it at the next gig, in Nottingham. There was no chance to run through the set beforehand, of course, to try out the new order. We had to go into it cold, with the list of songs taped up behind one of the keyboards in case our memories flipped.

I played it straight, like a kid in a party game. *Don't think about what you're going to do,* Christie had said. *Just let it happen.*

So I went out on to the stage with nothing in my head except the opening bars of 'Supernova'. It's not an easy song. We'd always made a point of being close together when we sang it, so that we could pick up our cues from each other and keep track of those cross-rhythms that sound so simple and are such pigs to sing. But now Christie was way over the other side of the stage, so far away that I had to concentrate my whole attention on his face, on his eyes and his mouth. I waited for the single sustained note from Job and then floated my first line across the stage, launching it as though it had to cross oceans and continents.

When Christie's answering bars came back, they made a link. An invisible cord that tightened as we sang, drawing the next notes out of me. And the next and the next. The audience felt it too and, for the first time on that tour, they responded to us. There's no mistaking that alertness, that special silence. It lifted me up and up, so that, as I pounded on from 'Lazy Jackson' to 'Living Over the Shop', I began to hear the blood thumping in my ears.

And all the time the space between me and Christie was shrinking and the charge was growing. He is so still on stage that I was hardly aware of him moving. His eyes stared at me almost without a blink and his body seemed to be the single motionless thing at the centre of all the noise. But all the time we drew nearer to each other, until we were together inside a bubble of sound that cut us off from everyone else in the theatre.

By the time we went into 'Break-out', I wasn't aware of anything except our voices, striding over the top of the band, carrying the melody, and my face, reflected very small in Christie's eyes. Everything else was a swirling darkness out of which music and applause thundered alternately. Pushing me higher up, deeper in.

Then we finished 'Break-out'. After a second or two of the audience's roar, Christie moved his head, giving the tiny, secret signal to begin 'Streatham Nights'. At the same time, he took the final step towards me, the intolerable step that made the distance between us too small and put him into my private space.

And it hit me. Like a bomb blast. I'd been expecting something *musical* to happen. A new improvisation perhaps that Christie and I would beat out at the climax of the song. But what clutched my throat and thudded into my body was something much more impossible, less manageable. I couldn't have sung at all if the rehearsal hadn't made it automatic.

I wanted to grab hold of him.

Oh, nothing coy. No romantic sighs and eye-fluttering. I just wanted to clutch him and hold him as close to me as I could, to bend my head and press my face into his shoulder. *Just let it happen!* There was no way, no way at all that I was going to give myself away like that, on stage, for the whole world to see. Oh, if I'd been small and pretty I might have done it and serve Christie right if he didn't like it. But as it was—I could just imagine the laughter.

And all the time the music was beating at me until, just for a second at the end, I did lose my voice and Christie's came over alone in the sudden silence, nasal and ironic.

'*. . . And it's not your guardian angel, girl. . . .*'

I breathed. I got the last notes out. And then Christie made to take another step towards me, closer than I could bear, daring me. My hands went out before I could stop them, gripping his shoulders, and the only way I could keep hold of Finch, the only way I could stop Janis Mary appearing up there on the stage for everyone to laugh at, was to shake and shake him and shake and shake. . . .

At the same moment, the song finished and the lights cut out. For a second I was locked into violence, digging my fingers into Christie's shoulders and shaking him in total darkness. Then my eyes adjusted and I saw Dave and Rollo coming to pull me off.

'For God's sake, Finch!' That was Dave, suffering from chauvinist shock. 'Are you crazy?'

Rollo grabbed my left hand, but his other arm was firm and steady round my shoulders. 'Are you all right,' he kept saying, 'are you all right?' And I didn't even know which of us he was talking to.

Then the lights were up and we turned to face real, full-blooded applause. But all I could think was, *Thank heaven we're not allowed an encore.* Rollo let go of me to wave at the kids, and I had to hold on to the mike stand to stop myself crumbling at the knees. Some things about yourself are hard enough to take, without discovering them in front of several thousand people. And it didn't help to have Christie at my elbow, as calm and untouchable as ever. As if it had never happened.

When we came off, Mae was in the wings. She'd come up from London specially that day. I think she was panicking because she'd heard bad things about her investment, but there was none of that now. Now she wasn't just a heavyweight boxer. She was World Champ, with glory in her eyes.

'Get cleaned up, you lot, and I'll stand you dinner at the Albany. Want a drink first?'

She's used to selling and all her performances are done cold, with one eye on the customer. She can't understand that it's impossible to step off-stage and click back to normal. Not when you're dripping sweat and dizzy from lack of oxygen. Luckily, Dave and Rollo were ready to suck up all the praise that was going, so they accepted the drink and swept Mae off to the dressing-room.

'*And* you, Christie,' murmured Job. 'I'll see to Finch.'

He steered me out of the wings, where we were being elbowed by the local band going on, and pushed me into a quiet corner. Job has a genius for finding spare space to be himself. He slumped down between coiled flexes and boxes of light bulbs and sat with his chin on his bent knees.

'Come on. Wind down, Finch.'

Carefully, as if my bones might splinter, I lowered myself to sit facing him. He fished in his pocket.

'Barley sugar? Good for shock.'

'Thanks.'

As I sucked it, he peered at me through the half-light of our hiding-place. 'Dangerous games,' he murmured. 'You could have given him concussion. Broken his neck.'

I crunched the barley sugar. 'Serve him right,' I said bitterly. 'He deserved it. He knew what would happen, didn't he?'

'I see,' said Job. 'You mean: You're *horrid* and I *hate* you.' The silly, besotted schoolgirl voice shut me up. I swallowed the rest of the barley sugar and looked away. 'Well?' he said. 'I'm right, aren't I?'

'It was obvious, was it?' I said at last. 'Because if it was, and everybody knows, I'll—'

'Oh come *on*. What are you going to do? Commit hara-kiri on-stage tomorrow night?' Job grinned suddenly. 'Stop sweating, Finch. Of course they don't all know. They'll go home and twitter, "The supporting band was *weird*. The singers *hated* each other and they ended up fighting." They'll never work out what it really was that made them sit up and listen.'

I swallowed. 'But Christie knows. Doesn't he?'

'So? What's new?' Job shrugged. 'What did you *think* he was setting up? I guess he'll be delighted with the way it's worked out, once his teeth have stopped rattling. He's probably dying to see how you'll react tomorrow.'

'You mean—he expects me to go through that again?'

'It worked, didn't it?'

'But it's not—it's *private.'* I looked down at my clenched fists. I can't use my feelings as a stage act.'

For a moment Job was quiet and I heard his breathing in between me and the muffled music thudding from the auditorium. Then he said. 'Look, when I joined Kelp, I had a wife and two kids. The band broke all that up, because when the choices came I chose the music. I don't even know where my family is now. So don't talk to me about privacy. It's not possible to keep things separate like that.'

'You could have left!' I said, startled into anger.

He gave a little, twisted smile and bounced it straight back at me. 'So can you. But if you stay, you have to give your best. No frontiers, Finch.'

Shutting my eyes, I imagined going up on stage night after night, opening myself up, knowing what would happen. 'Job, I *can't*—'

He grinned, disconcertingly. 'You can't lay into Christie like that every night, no. Even Christie's breakable. And there's no need to bash your feelings out. Violence can speak in whispers as well, you know. What you ought to do is provide yourself with—a substitute—in case you need it.'

'But I'm breakable too! It'll kill me. How can I go up there every night and split myself open so that people can see how much I—'

'Love him? Hate him?'

'Yes.' I said. 'Yes.' I felt sick. 'What am I going to *do?*'

Job stood up and looked down at me. 'You could try getting off the see-saw,' he said gravely.

Not easy to make bold new statements about Nitrogen Cycle when it's all been said before, but let's take our noses out of the air and admit that, even if their music's froth, Nikko and Shazz are real, hard professionals. On the first date of their new tour, they came on like fresh-minted daisies and had a disgruntled audience singing along football-fashion before I could blink twice.

From the first bars of *Don't Remember*, they lifted the gig out of the trough it had settled into. Amateurish sets from Kelp and Schizophrenia – even though they contained good material – had the audience restless and edgy and threatened to blight the whole evening, but they were quickly forgotten in the all-light all-colour show that Nitrogen Cycle have put together for this year's tour.

Rockwise: 13th July

I went to see Nitrogen Cycle in Nottingham and really enjoyed watching them perform live. But I nearly walked out before they came on, because we had to sit through not one but *two* supporting acts beforehand. The first one was particularly disturbing, because the two vocalists obviously hated each other like poison and there was nearly a fight on stage at the end of the set. I couldn't get them out of my mind for the rest of the evening. Why can't we have more bands as cheerful and sane and normal as Nitrogen Cycle?

Nikko's Crunchy Bar, Leeds.

You saw Nitrogen Cycle *live*, Crunchy Bar? Well, congratulations. Thought they couldn't perform unless someone wound up the clockwork.—No, seriously (well, almost!) it's rough being on stage as a supporting group when the whole audience just craves to have you off a.s.a.p. (If you see what I mean—whoops!)

Smash Hits: 19th-26th July

Ipswich Evening Star: 21st July

It was a strange evening at the Gaumont Theatre, in a bill that seemed to run backwards from hypertension to jolly jingles. Kelp, the unknown band who opened the show, had the audience wound up to a feverish pitch in twenty minutes or so, with their strong, startling songs. Some loved it, some hated it, but there were no neutrals by the final number, *Streatham Nights* (which was recently released as the group's first single). I had heard rumours (yes, even here in Suffolk!) that their set sometimes culminates in violence between the two vocalists and, having experienced the tension they generate, I can well believe it. But last night, more subtly and just as shockingly, Finch (that's her, not him, for the benefit of the uninitiated) ended by tearing a huge poster of the group, right across the picture of Christie's face. (That's him, not her.) Sounds comic? Well I shuddered, let me tell you. It was no act, and the message was that it could just as easily have been his face. This group is for *real*. Just like its music.

In comparison, our own Electric Cable had a hard time making an impression. . . .

Ipswich Evening Star: 21st July

Is Lionel Fram of Nobody's Business setting out to add a dash of culture to the group's hell-raising image? He was spotted last night sneaking into the Nitrogen Cycle gig at Newcastle City Hall with jetsetting pop poetess Annabee Briggs. *Lionel Fram at a Nitrogen Cycle gig?* Relax fans. When we challenged him, Lionel said, 'You don't suppose we came to listen to Nitrogen Cycle, do you?' And, having had a peek at Annabee's curvaceous shirt-front, we can well believe that they had better things to do. Poets aren't all skinny and lily-white. . . .

The Sun: 23rd July

Nitrogen Cycle/ Feet First/Kelp

The cream of the kindergarten were out in force to drool over luscious Shazz and would-be macho Nikko, and I expected that their usual imitation of Nureyev singing Mike Batt would be preceded by a largely plastic bill, suitable for the teenies and geriatrics who like to nod to N.C. But hang on! Way down in the jungle at the bottom of the bill, something stirred, and unknowns Kelp—catapulted into the dustbin position by the temporary crackup of Racing Demon—let some harsh fresh air into the doll's house. Two and a half weeks into Nitrogen Cycle's much-hyped tour, little but bad noises had come our way and we'd tottered into the Hippodrome complete with ear-plugs and nightcaps, ready to YAAAWN through the evening—when, lo and behold, Kelp split the gig wide open in the first half-hour with an incredibly impressive set.

From the silky menace of *Supernova* to the ear-pounding bitterness of *Streatham Nights*, it was quality rock all the way, with a growing tension that had the grannies and kiddies twitching in their chairs. No attempt—thank God!—at tarting the music up with fancy dress or stage tricks. Just a gradual, extraordinary build-up of electricity between the two singers that peaked, at the climax of *Streatham Nights*, in a slow, twisting destruction of one of the mike stands which made me feel I was watching a throttling. Fact or fiction? I certainly couldn't sort it out, but I expect to have plenty of chance with this intriguing band.

Feet First, on the other hand, should have gone out that way, and fast. A human audience, instead of one packed with doting relatives and robots, would have seen to it after the first two songs . . .

Sounds: 28th July

Chapter 13

And then Job wrote 'Face it'. I guess it was Lionel Fram's visit that sparked that off, although I've never asked. It was enough of a shock to start an earthquake. When we came off-stage in Newcastle he appeared within ten minutes, completely out of the blue. Just poked his head round the dressing-room door and grinned at us.

'Ker-ream!'

Then he was inside, bottle of whisky under one arm and Annabee Briggs under the other, without waiting for an invitation. Draping himself over the only real chair, he waved the bottle at us.

'Man, they all loved you out front. Loved you and hated you and wanted to *know* about you. I don't envy Nikko and Shazz tonight. That audience are going to find them about as exciting as a burst balloon.'

It blitzed us for a moment. You don't digest a visit from *Lionel Fram* in thirty seconds, especially not when you're still groggy from performing.

Christie recovered first. 'Sorry,' he said. Very cool. Refusing to be patronized. 'I don't seem to have caught your name.'

It wasn't a joke and Lionel didn't take it as one. He put the bottle down and was just shaping up for a bit of aggro when Annabee sat on him. Literally.

'Splat,' she said. 'Serve you right for playing the mega-star, sugarpuss. This lot don't need any pats on the head from us. They'll be in a position to do their own patting before you can turn round.' Removing the whisky bottle, which was jerking round perilously as he tried to heave her off, she held it out to Rollo. 'Got any glasses, cherub?'

Rollo scampered off to scrounge some, of course. That's Annabee all over. She's got a crazy, cute image, but that's just camouflage for a tough lady. I've never seen her waste more than five minutes before taking charge of a situation. By the time Rollo got back, she'd discovered who wrote our songs, got the rest of us started on a funny, fast slanging attack on Nitrogen Cycle, and peeled Job away into a corner. And Job, who never bothered much with strangers, was talking full tilt, his face pale and private, the way it looked when he was song-writing.

'. . . dangerous. . . .' I heard him say once. And '. . . but if it's spelt out, it's dead, isn't it? The whole point is the ambiguity, the tease. . . .'

'You're not going to give me all that garbage about "art" and "life", are you?' Annabee's voice was clear and carrying. 'You *must* know that they're the same thing. What do you think is going *on* when you're on-stage?'

I couldn't hear a word of Job's reply, but it made her laugh.

'Come on, chicken. You don't need me to give you lessons. You know all about taking risks.'

Dave sniggered and spluttered into his whisky and Lionel smacked his hand. 'Don't go thinking naughty thoughts about Annabee or she'll knock your teeth out. She always gets things the way she wants them. What do you think brought us here?' He laughed as Rollo's face fell about twenty feet. 'You thought it was me that came to see you, did you? No, I'm la-azy. Wouldn't cross the street to hear anyone. It was Annabee that heard about you and dragged us up here. She's really into performance.'

'Heard about us?' Christie and I said it together, but he didn't look towards me or grin, the way anyone else would have done. Ever since Nottingham, we'd hardly been speaking off-stage. When you get so close in public, it's hard to handle in private.

Lionel looked at us in amusement and then took a swig from the bottle. 'Just a distant rumble. But the jungle drums have got hold of your name all right. You could be heading for a big break—*if* you can dodge the anacondas and the tigers and the giant ants in the undergrowth.'

'And *if* you've got the guts to take a chance,' Annabee said, with a fierce look at Job. 'Oh, I could almost write it myself, if I knew—' And then she tossed her head back in a swirl of lemon-yellow hair and squawked with laughter.

Those two were exotic jungle creatures themselves. Lionel, long and brown and lazy, flopped sideways across the chair like a snake, as if he had joints every inch. And Annabee was a gorgeous, raucous parakeet, flying circles in the air above him. Different strategies, but the same bright, bright eyes and the same knack of keeping their own pace in the jungle world they moved in.

That was why they were sitting in our dressing-room. Not to help us or encourage us, but to be in at the beginning of something new that just might be big enough to affect them. It was better than any flattery and after they went we spent the evening almost reeling about. Not from the whisky, either.

Job wouldn't tell us what he and Annabee had been talking about, even though Dave teased and worried at him for hours. He shrugged and spread his hands and looked the other way, warning us off. But after the Edinburgh gig the next night, he vanished. Just lit out and disappeared for the whole of the rest day that followed.

Dave was the one who panicked. He dragged the rest of us round Edinburgh from Murrayfield to Holyrood and back, hunting in every café and cinema and pub. But we never found out where Job had been. He just turned up the next day in our dressing-room in Blackpool Winter Gardens, strolling in at half-past two in the afternoon.

'Cutting it a bit fine,' Christie said, before Dave could start.

Job nodded, apologetic but not grovelling. 'Sorry. It wouldn't come right until I got the idea of the rap. But it's O.K. now. Here.' He tossed a cassette on to the table and then looked at me. Oddly. 'I don't know what you'll make of it, but give it a listen and see—' His eyes weren't quite focusing and he was beginning to sway on his feet. For a second longer he hunted around for the right word and then he brushed the sentence aside with his hand and tapped the cassette. 'I'm sorry. O.K.? Just listen.'

Christie looked down and touched the black plastic with the tip of one finger, as if it was hot. 'So what is it?'

'It,' Job said. The fine lines round his eyes were deeper and black-smudged. 'The song we need. Now lay off. I've got to get some sleep before this evening.' Flinging his jacket into a corner of the room, he lay down with his head on it and before anyone could say a word he was asleep.

Dave bent down and covered him over with Rollo's yellow coat. 'Go and scrounge a tape-recorder from somewhere, Rollo,' he said over his shoulder.

Rollo dithered. 'Don't you think the noise—'

'He won't wake now. Not for a couple of hours.' Dave stood up. 'Oh, go on. He'll be furious if we haven't heard it by the time he comes round.'

Christie gave it the nod and Rollo trotted off in his usual docile way. We all stood staring at the cassette until he came back, as if somehow we already knew, and Christie glanced at me once or twice in a way that made my skin prickle. And yet I don't see how he can have had any idea of what sort of song Job had written.

The song. It's hard for me to remember now what it was like sitting in that dressing-room, with Job huddled in the corner, and hearing the opening bars for the first time, without knowing exactly what was coming.

'Came out of Birmingham with nothing. . . .'

Not like you're imagining, of course, with the harmonica and then the drums. Just Job's thin, harsh voice sketching in the tune and a tinny old piano to block out the instrumental parts. I don't know where he'd managed to make the recording, but the acoustics were terrible and he can't have had the proper equipment. He'd had to record one track on top of another to do the melody and the rap at the same time, and the hiss was so bad that the words of the rap were mostly lost. We had to concentrate quite hard just to get the general impression.

And yet. I can still feel the shudder that went up my back when the rhythm broke and he went into the chorus.

'Put your body where your mind is. . . .'

A double shudder. Half of me was clocking up the fact that the thing was spot-on. There's no mistaking that eerie tingle you get when something's a hundred (and one?) per cent right.

But the other half of me was registering that it was my own story. No attempt at disguise, no pretence of being fair to anyone. And Job had done it. *Job,* who knew exactly how I felt about that sort of thing. He was singing my life, offering it to the band in the best tune he'd ever written, and the others were watching me sideways, waiting to see what I would say.

I think I would have stopped it then and there, if I'd had any reason to think Mum cared about me any more. If she'd answered my letter or come to the Birmingham gig or—But, as things were, I just went on listening with the others, taking in the song.

Heat. Heat and anger. That's what I remember about recording 'Face It'.

After the tour, we really needed a break to get our energies back and review what had happened to the band, but that wasn't on offer. Zombie were crazy to get an album out, to capitalize on the publicity from the tour, and they leapt at the idea of putting out 'Face It' as a single from the album. So, within a couple of days of unpacking our suitcase, we were into intensive rehearsals, with the recording dates booked and uncomfortably close.

Ever wondered how toothpaste feels being squeezed out of a tube? Or what it would be like to be put through a combine harvester, in slow motion? With the air so hot and humid all the time that you could hardly breathe and four other people watching you and waiting for your voice to crack *again* and land them with an even longer session.

No, I'm not exaggerating. It really was that bad. You try putting yourself up in front of other people and singing—with all the truth that's in you and no holding back—

'When your flesh and blood don't give a damn. . . .'

when it's true, and you've spent hours wondering *why* she didn't write and *why* she never came. Or

'Put your body where your mind is. . . .'

when you've spent a whole tour trying to stop yourself doing just that. Trying to keep away from Christie and squash out the thoughts in your head.

And if that all sounds like chaos—well, it was. Mae called into a rehearsal after a couple of days, to see how we were shaping up, and she was appalled. Stood in the middle of the room and yelled at Christie, 'I can't even listen to it! The whole thing's a mass of jagged edges, and Finch sounds ready for carting off to a padded cell.' She zipped round at me. 'What are you letting them put over on you? You must have lost half a stone in the last couple of weeks and your face looks like junket. Why don't you hit back at them?'

No sympathy, notice. Nothing of the mother-figure about Mae. She wanted me up and battling, or she couldn't care less about me. If she'd been kind, I think I might have wept on her shoulder and begged a week's holiday, but all she wanted was Finch, so it was Finch that spat back at her.

'Why don't you get your nose out of here? How do you expect to know what's going on if you swan in and listen to a couple of minutes in the middle of rehearsal? Just let us sort it out ourselves.'

'Yeah, piss off, Mae,' Christie said amiably. 'Come back *next* week. Then we'll have everything straight and I'll tell you what I want to do about the video for "Face It".'

For a moment I thought there was going to be an explosion. Mae had invested a lot of money in us by then, and I guess Stanley was beginning to lean on her, wanting to see some return. And there we were throwing her out. Christie let her come to the boil for a few seconds, so we all got the feel of the situation. Then he said gently, '*You've* got to trust *us* too, Mae. We let you have your way about the tour. Now we need to be right.'

She took the message. I could see the anger behind her eyes start to damp down and after swallowing a couple of times she even managed a smile.

'You lot bite everything, don't you? Even the hand that feeds you. O.K. Seven days. And I'll be back—' she checked her watch '—half-past eleven exactly. Right?'

'Right,' Christie said. And grinned.

Then she went. But somehow the balance of the rehearsal had shifted. I don't know if it was the adrenalin in my blood or a change in the temperature outside, but I seemed to have taken a step away from the raw stuff of the song. Instead of being Janis Mary, in it up to the neck, I could be Finch, feeling it but singing and not drowning.

'You see, the point is that it's true,' I said to Ida some time late that night. 'A band's not a machine, It's the combination of the people in it, and we're putting all that into the album. Especially "Face It".'

'The Royal Philharmonic Orchestra is people as well,' Ida said. 'But they don't play *their* life stories.'

'Who cares about them?' I finished my cup of cocoa and wondered whether to make some more, even though it was still sweating-hot. Somewhere along the way, I'd got a taste for the filthy stuff. 'But bands like ours can't separate the music from the people. They're all part of the same thing.'

'So you mince yourself into little pieces just to entertain an audience?' Ida said dryly. Somewhere along the way she had changed too, I thought. Five months ago, she wouldn't have noticed if I came down with smallpox, but now she was looking really worried. She leaned across the table and put a hand on my arm. 'Take care of yourself, Janis. Because Chris won't do it for you. If he thinks his precious band needs your blood, he'll have the tube in your arm before you can blink.'

At least he'd have to look at me then.

Oh no, I didn't say it out loud. I wasn't quite as far gone as that. But those weeks were so heavy and hot and crazy that for a second I did actually think I wouldn't mind giving up a pint or two of blood to get Christie to look at me in an ordinary, human way, without a microphone in his hand.

I stood up so quickly that I jarred the table. 'I need some sleep.' Ida drooped a bit, so I gave her a quick pat on the head. 'Don't fret about me. I can stand up to a lot, you know. Anyway, I think the worst of it's over. Things are beginning to fall into place.'

I was right in a way, because we never had another rehearsal as bad as the one Mae had interrupted. 'Face It' came together almost at once the next day and there was no problem with the other songs, of course. But the real gold-plated, blood-tingling row was still to come.

Philip Tissiman. Oh, we'd known all along that Zombie had signed him up to produce the album, and I hadn't thought twice about it, although I'd heard Job and Christie muttering about him. But we should have guessed that we couldn't push him around. He's a nice guy, young and earnest and very quiet, but you don't get to the top without being a bit more complicated than that, and he had a reputation of his own to maintain.

The trouble came the minute we began to discuss 'Face It'. At least, Philip called it 'discussing', but he really meant that he was giving us our instructions about the session. We'd been docile and awed by his fame and his professionalism when we did 'Streatham Nights' and I suppose he expected the same treatment this time. Anyway, he didn't ask opinions. Just told us how we were going to record the song.

'I'd like to start with the drum track and then lay down the rap beside that, to get those two clear before we go on to—'

'No,' said Job, very stiffly. 'No, we can't do it like that Philip. The whole lot's got to be recorded together. Close-miked.'

Philip stopped dead. He's one of those people who talk with their hands and for a moment they were stuck in mid-air on their own. 'I *beg* your pardon,' he said. Sounding as if he was speaking out of solid ice instead of through sweltering heat.

Christie moved up behind Job. 'We've talked it over. It's got to be a single recording, Philip.'

'But you know I don't work like that. It's messy and inaccurate—'

'We need that sort of feel for this song,' Job said. 'It's got to feel authentic. Feel it and sound it and *smell* it. There's no room for anything artificial. We've got to have the roughness—'

'It'll be rough, all right,' Philip said. He was breathing harder and he ran a finger round inside the neck of his loose T-shirt as if it choked him. Then he had a go directly at Christie. 'Look, you won't like it. You like things sharp and clean and accurate, just as much as I do. How do you think we're going to get that kind of perfection if—'

'It's *not* perfect if it's wrong for the song, is it?' Christie said stubbornly. 'And the song's what matters, not the recording.'

'It's not that drastic,' Job said, soothingly. 'If we can just go through—'

'You can just go through the bloody *ceiling!*'

I've never seen anyone blow up so fast. One minute he was the Philip we knew, angry but recognizable, and the next he was shaking and yelling.

'All you little bands are the same! Make one single and you think you're experts. Well, you can produce your *own* record if you want to piddle about. I'm not a mechanic, I'm an artist, and if you don't want my contribution—'

The words poured out like hot lava for two or three minutes, while his face twisted and his voice got shriller and shriller. Weird. Then he stamped out, banging the door behind him.

It wasn't just us, of course. He was only a month away from his second nervous breakdown, and that disagreement was the match to a whole lot of tinder of his own that was making him obsessively meticulous. But we certainly provided the spark, there was no question about that.

'What did you *do* to the man?' Mae said furiously. 'What's the point of having someone like him and then not taking his advice—?'

'He's *wrong,'* Job said patiently. 'About this song. We don't want it faked up, and we *can* do a perfect, one-off performance of it, because we're that sort of band. You know we are, Mae. And this song's *got* to be real.'

She looked at us, her bright black button-eyes going snap-snap-snap from face to face, taking in the fact that we were all agreed. Even Dave, who never fussed about anything except his own part. Even Rollo, who hated upsetting people. 'Zombie *are* very keen on this real-life angle,' she said slowly. 'On doing the video in the actual café and so on. If you really feel that Philip's not an appropriate person to produce the record—'

'Yes.' Job and Christie said it together. Firmly.

'So who do you want?'

The two of them looked at each other and then Job said, in a voice that showed how far he was pushing his luck, 'Alan Sidelski.'

'What?' Mae stared for a moment and then she laughed. 'What's this? The managers' Olympics?' She stood up. 'O.K. I'll see what I can do.'

Heaven knows how she swung it, but we were back in the studio with Alan Sidelski by the end of the next week. We'd lost our booking, though, so we had to go in in the middle of the night once or twice and that's how 'Face It' was finally recorded. With all of us feeling battered and exhausted from the rehearsals and rows, Alan yelling and screaming in the way he always does when he's working, and the rest of the world asleep and dreaming. And even at that time of night it was sweltering hot, with the heaviness of hovering thunder.

Chapter 14

You have to remember all that chaos to imagine how we felt by the time the single was released. You have to remember that it came after the tour, and Lionel Fram, and those terrible rehearsals, and Philip Tissiman, and the midnight sessions in the studio. The world had tilted off balance for all of us and the only thing that kept us upright, like a lifeline, was our determination that 'Face It' wasn't going to sink without trace, like 'Streatham Nights'.

If you can keep all that in mind, perhaps you'll understand what happened with me and the Rat.

It could only have been Rat Saunders, of course. Tell someone you didn't recognize Mike Read or Peter Powell and they'd laugh themselves into next week. All those other Radio One D.J.s get their faces everywhere—decorating T.V. shows, judging knobbly knees contests, printed on T-shirts and tattooed on sailors. Rat Saunders is the only one who's never put himself about like that. Just the one show. And the massive, *monumental* clout that goes with being listened to by eight out of ten teenagers across the country every week.

I *did* know what he looked like, actually, but even then, when I saw him sitting in a dark corner of the pub, with his legs blocking the doorway to the Ladies, I wasn't quite sure. The rest of the band were playing darts in the other bar and I was all on my own (heading for that doorway) when I saw his long, bony face and the idea came to me.

Six months before, it would have been a wild notion to fantasize about while I squeezed past his feet, keeping my eyes down in case he thought I was gawping at him. I'd have passed up my chance and then sat in the bog dreaming about how wonderful it would be if he noticed our record. But I guess I was used to *making* things happen by then. I didn't think Finch would waste a chance like that. So I charged across the bar, tripped over his feet and landed smack against the solid wooden door beyond him.

Oh, I was all right. Falling was the first thing Bernard ever taught me and there was no way I was going to hurt myself. But I made certain that the flat of my hand hit the wood hard, and I came up with my fingers rubbing my jaw and my teeth bared.

'What do you think you're doing, sitting sprawled out like that? Think the whole pub belongs to you? You'll need it if you've damaged my face, because I'll sue you for all you're worth.'

The apologetic look vanished from his face. 'Come on now.' His voice was even colder that it sounds on the radio. And he didn't look any more attractive. Imagine an under-ripe banana with a small moustache. 'Your face is hardly worth that much.'

'My face is my *living,*' I said fiercely. 'Especially my mouth.'

He got that all right. He'd guessed what I was. But he wasn't letting on. 'What are you, then? A bingo caller?' It was the frosty-voiced push-off. 'Don't give me that. Your face is perfectly all right.'

'Want me to stay here so you can watch it swell?' I snapped. 'Look at you. You haven't even moved your *feet!*' And I bent down and heaved them up in the air, sending him sliding about in his chair, so that he had to grip the sides to stop himself being flung on to the floor. *Very* undignified. And you could tell from his face that he hated it. I dumped the feet on the table.

'Now, let's have your name and address,' I said. 'Or do I get the landlord to call the police?'

His eyes flickered as he tried to work out whether or not I was faking. Then he shrugged and flicked a card across the table. 'O.K. Send your solicitor round when you've got some good bruises to show me. But they'd better be good.'

I held the card in my hand and made myself count to five while I looked down at it.

Rat Saunders
The Hits and the Pits
BBC Radio One

What did I do? Faked-up astonishment would have come across as pure plastic. I let my face go stony and tried to get over the small, sick shudder of finding that I really had been right about who it was. Then I went on playing Finch.

'Great. Wonderful.' My voice was bitter. 'You can really get your own back, can't you?'

He raised one black eyebrow. 'Oh?'

'Don't play innocent.' I slapped the card down fiercely on the table. 'After all the effort we put into that album—especially 'Face It'—and now you can kill the whole lot off. Just because I didn't meekly let you trip me up.'

He snatched the card up and slipped it back into his pocket. 'I wouldn't have known you had anything to do with the music business, would I? Not if you hadn't made a point of telling me.' He was suspicious now, all right.

'Oh sure you wouldn't! Look, my face is all over the record sleeve. Are you going to tell me I'm so ordinary that you wouldn't know it again?' I stepped past him and opened the door. 'Well, if you want a nice, cheap little revenge you know where to get it. I'm Finch, and I'm not going to grovel to anyone.'

Banging through the door, I locked myself into a cubicle and sat there shivering. He'd notice us all right now. If our single got anywhere near him, he was bound to listen to it, out of curiosity if nothing else. But had I gone too far and fouled everything up?

When I came out, the Rat was standing waiting for me. He's as tall as I am, and he looked me hard in the eyes.

'Swallow this,' he said stiffly. 'I'll listen to your record with a perfectly open mind. The same as I listen to all the new releases. Nobody can do anything to shake that—a bunch of flowers would be just the same as a hysterical tantrum. I'm impartial.'

'O.K.' I was too startled to dredge up any other reply, but inside my head I was beginning to grin. So that was his weak point, was it? His precious reputation for impartiality. As he turned and walked off, I was thinking to myself that things were stacked in our favour now. Having someone trying not to be biased against you is almost as good as having someone biased in your favour. It took me two or three minutes to get rid of the grin so that I could race back into the other bar and play at being innocent.

'—why didn't one of you morons *tell* me what Rat Saunders looks like?'

I'm not sure any of them believed me. Except Rollo, of course. But Christie made sure we would be around to hear the Rat's next programme.

And Rollo's mum turned the whole thing into a party. 'Don't be stupid,' she said, in her usual cheerful way. 'Of course he'll play it. Hasn't it been on the radio a couple of times already? It's a brilliant song and being played by the Rat will send it straight to the top.'

'*Mum—*' Rollo shook his head at her. He's too superstitious to care for that sort of talk and he was touching wood like mad. His mother tweaked his ear.

'Look, why don't you all come round here to listen to the programme? I'll cook up a pile of spare-ribs and make a cake. No point in sitting in that disgusting flat chewing your fingers while the thing's on.'

And then, somehow, Rollo's sister and her fiancé were coming and Rollo decided we should ask Mae and Stanley. And Jed and Bernard too, as a way of thanking them. By the time Monday came, there were about twenty people expected. I borrowed a huge check shirt from Rollo and raced back to Ida's at five o'clock to have a bath. The last party I'd been to was Darling Chloe's and I wanted this one to be quite different.

Coming out of the bathroom wrapped in one towel and

rubbing my hair dry with another (that took about three minutes—almost made up for the time I had to spend at Jed's, getting it cut) I bumped into Ida and nearly tripped over her.

'There's a fresh pot of tea made, ' she chirped. 'And I've cooked a Swiss roll. We can—'

'Sorry.' I went on towelling my head. 'Got to go out.'

'But it's the programme.' She sounded puzzled. 'The one you told me about.'

'That's right.' I rubbed harder. Nearly dry. 'We're all going round to Rollo's to listen. His mum's laid on a bit of a party.'

Through the thickness of the towel over my head, I heard a small squeak. Lifting one corner to have a look, I saw Ida's expression. 'What on earth—?'

'Nothing.' She turned her head away and said it again, fiercely. '*Nothing!*'

'Oh sure. Come on, Ida. Spit it out.'

Dumb, dumb dumb! Fancy asking when she was actually trying *not* to tell. If I'd had any sense I would already have been in my room.

Ida sniffed. 'It's just—well, you told me how important this programme was, and you said you thought there was a chance—and I just thought it would be nice if we—oh, it doesn't matter.'

Droop, drip. Mum used to be an expert at it. Now I'd feel rotten whatever I did, because I either had to abandon Ida or miss out on the party. I knew how I ought to deal with it, the Finch way. A quick, crisp pat on the shoulder and 'I'll tell you all about it afterwards.' Not unkind, but not a doormat either.

Only—oh, poor old Ida. Sometimes I wanted to batter Christie for leaving her alone in that dark little house with nothing to do but think about the past. *Yes, of course I'll stay. That would be great.* The words almost leaked out before I saw the solution. Ridiculously easy.

'Cheer up, Ida,' I said. 'Go and jump into a party dress and put your Swiss roll in a tin. You can bring it along to Rollo's mum's.'

'Oh, I couldn't—'

I knew those yes-you-can-no-I-can't conversations, as well. If I got trapped into one of those, we'd spend all evening on the landing. Catching hold of her elbow, I pushed her into her bedroom and opened the wardrobe door.

'Right now. Which is your favourite dress?'

Black. With swansdown. But why argue if she was happy? I patted her hand.

'Great. I'll go and get dressed while you change. There should be a bus in about ten minutes.'

We missed that bus, of course. And the next one. By the time we arrived, the programme was just about to start and the room was jammed with people. I walked in, dragging Ida after me, and said, 'Anyone got a chair for Christie's mum?'

It was one of those magic, hilarious moments that you only remember afterwards, with everyone registering shock and trying to take in the new character—Finch the Good Samaritan. And all the time Ida was twittering, 'No really, the floor's all right,' and Christie was staring at me as though I'd suddenly turned green.

Then Rollo shouted, 'It's starting!' and heaved his sister out of an armchair to let Ida sit down, just as the familiar whispering voice said the familiar opening words:

'And now, with the Hits and the Pits—*it's the Rat.*'

No signature tune. No taped snippets of chat. Just the voice and straight into the first record, which was always something really scabby. One of the pits, not one of the hits. This time round, it was a sentimental ballad, turgid as old semolina, performed by a couple singing very slowly and rather flat. Poor Ida smiled and swayed from side to side in time to the music, with a lunatic smile on her face. She must have been the only person who'd never heard Rat Saunders before, and she was in for a nasty surprise.

Sure enough, when the song ended and he spoke, she went pink and peeped round to check if anyone had noticed her.

'Moving with the beat, were you?' said the harsh cold

voice from the radio. 'Wiping tears from your eyes while you looked for a bucket to be sick into? Well, you super-critical listeners, I'll thank you to remember that Nina and David *have* to sing their hearts out like that. Because their brains and their guts got lost, way back in the Stone Age and their ears were seriously damaged as well. Hearts are all they have. . . .'

Oh, it's a good formula for a programme. Half a dozen or so appalling records, usually by famous bands having an off-day, and all of them slashed to bleeding by the Rat, with his polite, poisonous tongue. And, tucked in between, the same number of new, unknown records that the Rat was tipping for the charts. That was why the kids all listened. The slaughter was funny—I can remember nearly choking once or twice, caught between laughter and cringing—but the good records were the core of the programme. Because the Rat was always right. His tips didn't always make the charts, but nine times out of ten they got into the top seventy-five and sometimes they did much, much better. If you missed listening to the Rat, you were always liable to find on Tuesday that everyone you knew was talking about a band or a singer that you'd never heard of. If he played 'Face It', we would instantly be off the bottom rung of the ladder, and thousands of people would go out and buy our record.

None of us enjoyed the programme that evening, of course, because we were far too tense. Ida looked more and more bewildered and finally settled for a frozen face and safety. The rest of us fidgeted, sat on our hands, bit our nails. As soon as a record began, we were wishing it to end, so that we could discover what the next one would be. A pity, really, because there were some good things on that week—Joel Langley's 'Deadline Friday' and The Hive's 'No Dice'—but afterwards I didn't even remember hearing them because I was too busy watching the clock on the mantelpiece, trying to work out how many more records the Rat would fit in.

At last he said, 'Now—rock bottom,' and we leaned back and pulled faces and tried to look as if we didn't care.

Except Rollo, who can't look anything except what he is. He said, 'Perhaps he'll play it next week,' hopefully, and idiotically, as if he didn't know that the Rat only played new releases.

'But there's another record yet,' Ida said, sounding puzzled.

Christie snapped at her. 'Oh shut up! It's only one of the funnies. Haven't you got any—'

Then he froze.

'. . . and why *not* use your life-story?' said the Rat's sour voice. 'I'm thinking of cashing in on this idea myself. If Kelp's large lead singer can shout her problems to the world and show them on video, then I can do it too. Watch out for the new Rat Saunders video *Face Zit* with real life scenes of me getting up in the morning. Fearless close-ups of me squeezing my spots! Detailed coverage of the state of my tongue! And I may even manage to scrape up a droning harmonica to accompany the flushing of the lavatory. But, even then, I don't suppose I'll make you squirm as much as this record will.'

We were fighting not to believe it, until the first notes of the harmonica took over from the Rat and my voice began (no, not shouting, I don't shout).

Came out of Birmingham with nothing. . . .

Christie leaped across the room and switched off the radio.

'*I* think it's a nice record,' Ida said.

Then even she got the message and her voice died away, leaving a terrible gap as we all waited for Christie's reaction. But he didn't move. He stayed stooped over the table, leaning heavily on his hands, with his back to us. The silence stretched out from one minute into two, until Stanley (of all people!) finally broke it.

'That was certainly hostile. But it's only one programme, of course, and someone else may—'

'It's not *only one programme,*' Dave interrupted rudely. 'It's the Rat, and he's killed 'Face It' stone dead. Probably killed Kelp as well. Why on earth didn't you manage to miss his feet, Finch and—'

'Shut up, bonehead!' Christie turned at last, with a stony, pale face. 'It's got nothing to do with his feet.'

He barged across the room, treading on fingers and toes and looking like I felt when Dad went, or when Mum brought Himmler home. As he passed Mae, she caught at his hand.

'No point in being suicidal about it, Christie. We ought to discuss if there's any way we can use this—'

'How about as an obituary?' he snapped, shaking off her hand. He turned and glanced over his shoulder, straight at me. 'Come on, Finch.'

No explanation. But I got straight up and followed him out to the van.

Chapter 15

He started the engine before I had settled into the passenger seat and we were off, into the dark, as I slammed the door. Without a word, he drove west, his face rigid and cold. I kept thinking, *If I touch it, my fingers will freeze* and I had to sit on my hands to stop them making the test.

Once, I switched the radio on, because the silence was beginning to sing in my ears and I didn't dare break it with my own voice, Christie just leaned forward and switched off again, without even a change of expression.

Once we stopped to buy petrol, just outside Guildford, and he said a single word.

'Money.'

When we turned out our pockets and put everything together, we had enough to buy fifteen gallons. Christie bought nine and kept the rest. Then we drove on in silence.

Just before midnight, we hit Bournemouth and he turned off the main road and plunged into suburban streets, weaving his way across the town until the houses ended. Beyond, a great hump of land reared up black in front of us, with the sea on both sides. Christie spun the car into a dark waste of car-park, pulled the keys out of the ignition and opened his door. Before I had time to open my mouth, he was out of the car-park and walking away.

It took me a couple of minutes to catch him up. When I did, he stopped and stood with his hands in his pockets, looking out over a stretch of black water. Little waves lapped in the darkness and, half a mile away, lights curved round on the other side of the bay.

'Well?' I said.

At first I thought he wasn't going to answer, but then he turned, suddenly fierce, and hissed at me:

'I was so *sure*. I could have sworn that everything about that record was right.'

Perhaps I might have understood more if I'd been able to see his face properly. But it was like being battered by an unexplained force. All I could do was wait for him to go on, and that turned his anger full on me.

'Oh, I suppose you're like the rest. Suppose you think I'm whining because we got bad marks from the Rat. Poor old Christie. Overreached himself and got his knuckles rapped.'

'I got my knuckles rapped too,' I said. 'Don't smother me with sympathy, will you?'

'That's nothing. *Nothing.*' He took hold of my shoulders and gripping hard, digging his fingers in. 'Look, Finch, we could always make another record. *Except that I thought this one was good.* If I'm wrong about that, I can't make another one. I don't know how to go about it. Understand now?'

'It *is* a good record,' I said. Not to comfort him, but because I believed it.

His shoulders hunched forward and he kicked at the path as he let go of me. 'The Rat's always right,' he said softly. 'You know that as well as I do. Every scabby band he slaughters probably thinks it's made a good record.'

'It *is* a good record,' I said again, but I don't think Christie even heard me. He slouched up the path, into the darkness, and as I followed him he began to talk in a low, harsh voice.

'We came to Bournemouth for holidays. When I was a kid. And I got bored with dragging round the shops and eating sandy sandwiches. I used to nag Dad to bring me here, so that I could ride on the little train that goes along to the end of the Head.'

A dark, sulky little boy with a bucket and spade, dragging his feet around department stores, kicking at sand-castles and generally making a pain of himself. I could see him clearly. But Christie wasn't doing the Happy

Snapshots of my Childhood bit. There was nothing sentimental about his voice.

'I adored that little train. Until I was seven. And when I was seven, Dad began to build the North Star, and I suddenly saw through the one here. Understood that it wasn't a real model, but just a toy for the dear little kiddies, with rubber tyres and not even a pretence of running on rails instead of the road.'

'Sad,' I said. Bewildered again.

'Don't be stupid,' Christie said scornfully. 'Of course it wasn't sad. It was wonderful. I felt fantastically grown-up, and I thought, *Now I understand about quality*. It's the first moment I remember being—myself. Not just a silly kid. And ever since then, I've trusted my own judgement, relied on the fact that I could pick out the best.' He stopped and stared out over the water. 'Until tonight.'

Oh Christie.

I don't know why I always thought of pity as a soft thing. It's savage, painful, unbearable, like a knife twisting in your stomach. I *did* see. I *did* understand. And there was Christie, hunched beside me in the darkness, so close that I could hear his breath catch in his throat, could reach out and touch him if I dared.

He turned towards me. 'Well?'

'Join the human race,' I heard my voice say harshly. 'What's so great about *you*, Christie Joyce, that you've got to be right all the time?'

His head jerked up as he slammed back at me. 'So I *was* wrong, was I?' he snapped. '"Face It" is as rubbishy as the Rat said it was?'

'Of course it isn't,' I snapped back '*You're* the one who was giving in, not me.'

'It's not rubbishy?'

'It's a great record.'

'Stupendous?' He was mocking me now.

'Yes!'

'Original?'

'Absolutely!'

'Heading straight for the top?'

'Of course!'

'Sure to win the Nobel Prize for—?' But he was laughing too much to go on and I began to laugh too, standing in the darkness with the sea wind skimming my face and the sleepy squawks of the water birds coming up from the reeds.

Christie punched me on the arm. 'At least I was right about *you*. If you'd gone soft on me just then, I think I would have jumped into the harbour.' While I was still wondering whether that was a compliment I wanted, he was starting back down the path. 'Come on. Let's see if there's anything to eat in the van.'

'For Heaven's sake, Christie! It's one o'clock in the morning.'

'Blow that!' He was suddenly wild, like a kid let out of a tedious exam. 'You've been slogging your guts out for six months—and I've had three years of it. Let's break the rules, Finch. We'll stay here and have a holiday.'

'You're crazy!' I loped after him. 'We've hardly got any money, there are things arranged for us to do—'

'*But no one knows where we are.* And we've got the van to sleep in and enough money to buy chips. Come on.'

You can buy a lot of chips for ten pounds. For three days, Christie and I ate nothing else. We tramped along the beach and wandered round the shops, nibbling chips out of paper bags and talking, talking, talking.

Not about the Rat, though. He went out of bounds as a subject for conversation when we wandered into a record shop to look at that week's new charts. The last charts that were made up before the Rat had played our record. The moment we walked into the shop, we saw 'Face It' propped in the stand. A new entry, at Number Thirty-Eight.

For a moment, I actually thought I was going to be sick. We'd done it, we'd actually got into the Top Forty—and it was no use. The Rat had splatted us, even before the charts were released. I gripped tight hold of a rack full of golden oldies and swallowed hard.

Then Christie touched my arm. When I looked up, he grinned and jerked his head towards the door. 'We're on holiday. Remember?'

And that was it. We left the shop and didn't go near another place that sold records all the time we were there. It was as if we had an unspoken agreement not to mention Zombie or Mae or anything to do with the music business.

But if you think that means we stopped talking about *music,* then you don't know Christie. He couldn't stop talking about music even if all the people he knew were stone deaf. He buried himself (and me) in endless technical discussions about the songs. We argued until we were exhausted, all day and far into the night, until Christie ushered me firmly into the front seat of the van and curled himself up in the back. He didn't care where we were or who was listening. The music was all that mattered.

'Here,' he said suddenly, on Wednesday, in the middle of all the shoppers crowding the Square. 'Listen to this.' And he launched into the last section of 'Supernova' at the top of his voice, stamping his feet to explain something he wanted to change about the drum part.

And on Thursday, when we were half-way up the pier, I made a careless remark about the rhythm of 'Lazy Jackson'.

'Well, go on, then,' Christie said. 'I don't think it'll work, but let's hear what you mean.'

So I stood and sang the whole song, letting the music float out over the darkening sea. Terrifying the sea-gulls flying home to bed. Christie was right, of course, and it didn't work, but I think that if I could deep-freeze one moment of my life, to have it back whenever I wanted, it would be that one. You know what I mean? *I felt as if I could burst out singing.* Well, I was even beyond that. I *was* singing, tying my tonsils in knots while Christie laughed at me, alone with him on an island in time where nobody could reach us.

That evening, we parked the van so that we could look

out over the sea and we sat side by side in the front seat, eating our chips. Not looking at each other, not speaking, but so close that I could feel the different rhythms of our breathing. Six of my breaths to five of his. All the music had stopped now. No melody, no harmony, just that difficult cross-rhythm, five against six. And slowly, barely noticeably, my breathing grew faster until it was five against seven and I knew he must have sensed the difference.

'Christie—' I said.

He picked the empty chip bag out of my lap and looked straight at me for a moment, his face very stern and solemn in the dim light.

'I know,' he said.

Then he was out of the van, crumpling the chip bags in his hands. Dropping them into a litter-bin, he stood alone on the edge of the sea for a minute or two, staring out into the darkness. Then he walked back towards the van and opened the doors at the back.

'That's the end of the chips, Finch,' he said. Quite gently for him. 'We're skint.'

I don't know what I said, but I must have made some odd kind of noise because he went on in a rougher voice.

'I don't know about you, but I'm sick of chips. It's time to go home.'

The next morning, we squeezed into a phone-box and put a reversed charge call through to Mae's office. She came on to the line like a bomb.

'Where *are* you?'

'Far away on a sunny tropical beach,' Christie said.

'Is Finch with you?'

'I'm sitting in her pocket,' Christie said, pulling a rude face at me.

'Put her on.'

We should have guessed something was wrong, from the sharpness in her voice, but our minds were still half on holiday. I pulled a face back at Christie and shook my head.

'What's it worth, Mae?' he said.

For a good ten seconds, she stopped talking altogether, letting the silence make her point. Then she said, very quiet and grim, 'Let me talk to Finch, please Christie.'

'Yes?' I called down the phone, as Christie pressed the receiver to my ear. 'It's me.'

'Listen, Janis—'

I think the world changed at that one word. Mae never called me Janis. 'Cut out the jam,' I said, too afraid to be polite. 'What's the matter?'

'O.K., then. I'll tell you straight.' And I heard her take a long, deep breath.

Kimber

Peacefully in hospital on Wednesday 31st October, Barbara Anne, much loved wife of Graham and mother of Janis. Funeral service on Tuesday 6th November at the Central Crematorium at 11.00 am. Family flowers only, please, but donations, if desired to Cancer Research.

Birmingham Post, 2nd November

Chapter 16

Aha!

Oh, I can almost feel you prick your ears up now the story's getting on to familiar ground. You think you know what's coming, don't you? You're remembering all those grey, blurred photographs of me looking pale and haggard and the corny headlines over them.

SUCCESS COMES TOO LATE

'MUM NEVER KNEW!' SAYS FINCH

I bet you believed the heart-wrenching version too, didn't you? Thought I went off to the funeral all unsuspecting and got hit by the good news right out of the blue. But of course it wasn't like that. Just give it a bit of thought and you'll see that it can't have been. However fast a single goes up the charts, it can't be a total surprise, because the actual records have to come from *somewhere*. And that means someone's bound to notice. So, from the moment Christie and I got back from Bournemouth and walked into Mae's office we knew that something weird and unexpected had happened.

It seems to have come out of nowhere—from the street. Suddenly, everywhere, the mesage was getting round: *the Rat's finally boobed!* And everyone wanted the record that had spoilt his super-perfect reputation for being right. Sales of 'Face It' took off like a moon-shot and Zombie were going crazy pressing and re-pressing it.

But they didn't just scramble to keep up with the demand. They *used* the situation, and we began to understand what had made them so successful. The minute they got a sniff of what was up, they had thousands of little stickers printed, showing the face of a weeping rat, and they slapped them on to the record sleeves. Then they started selling rolls of the stickers to the public. By the Friday, rat stickers were appearing all over the place.

Even Lionel Fram. He turned up out of the blue on Saturday with little rats plastered all over his shoes. We had a couple of hours talking to him at the flat and he invited us to a party the week after. He must have been spreading the word, as well, because there was a tiny rat scrawled in one corner of the postcard we got on Monday, from Annabee Briggs, in Fiji.

Fantastic, marvellous, what a great record!
I'm playing it all over Suva and it's driving them wild. Told you you could do it!
Annabee

No mistaking those signals. The people who made it their business to be at the sharp end had homed in on us.

So I knew. But the problem was caring. I could feel all the others watching me—Mae, Christie and the rest of the band—wanting me to share their eagerness to hear the new charts on Tuesday, to see exactly how we were doing. And I tried, I really tried to care, but it all seemed distant and unreal.

Once, right in the middle of Mum's worst depression, I came home from school and found the house empty. The whole place was a huge echo chamber, as hollow as if burglars had got in and stripped it bare. Standing in the hall, I shouted for her in a panic, wondering what would happen if they really had taken her away. But then her footsteps sounded on the path and suddenly she was there, with her arms full of hot fish and chips, fetched in for a treat because she was having a good day.

No fish and chips now, not ever again. I was rattling round on my own in the emptiness, as if I was trapped in that hollow house with no one but an echo to answer me. Unable to understand the faces that peered in through the windows, mouthing nonsense about record sales and radio coverage.

Everything was meaningless except the fact that Mum's funeral was on Tuesday. The day we were all waiting for. The day that seemed as though it would never come.

And then, all in a rush, it was there. I got up very early in the morning to catch my train and Christie drove me to Euston in the van. It was the first time we had been alone together since we got back from Bournemouth, but I was still too numb to care who I was with and I don't remember speaking to him at all on the way. I just stared through the windscreen while he glanced sideways at me. As he pulled up to let me out, he murmured, 'Want me to phone?'

'What?' I really didn't know what he was on about.

'Do you want me to phone you when the charts come out?'

I think I must have looked too surprised to speak, because he gazed at me for a moment and then shrugged and drove off, leaving me to catch the train on my own. I made it with ten minutes to spare and, once I stepped into the carriage, I had left London. All my thoughts were in Birmingham.

It seemed obscene that Himmler was still going to be in the house. It was Mum's house, Mum's and mine. As I sat staring out of the window, watching the stations tick by (. . . Watford, Milton Keynes, Rugby, Coventry . . .) I wiped him out and let my mind float back to the time before he barged in. The time just after Dad lit out, when money was tight and it was me and Mum on our own. My little Mum, who needed coaxing and bullying to keep her out of the black glooms. I'd done it, too. I'd wheedled her into carrying on, when she was ready to lie down and give up—and now she was dead, and it was all for nothing.

And Himmler was waiting in the empty house, playing the poor, bereaved husband. Sob. Everyone would sympathize with him, because he was the one who'd married her, and I was only the daughter who'd taken her money and run away. Not satisfied with having her while she was alive, he would have to be chief mourner now she was dead.

Why couldn't she wait for me to come home and explain?

Walking up the path, I pulled out my keys, automatically, and my hand had almost reached the keyhole before I remembered. Himmler's house now. I rang the bell.

When he opened the door, I felt myself shrivel. He'd made himself into a cartoon of a grieving husband, with bags under his eyes and shrunken, yellowish skin. Even his moustache was drooping.

'Hi,' I said.

'Hallo, Janis.' His voice was duller than I expected. 'Come in.'

I stepped across the threshold. From the lounge, I could hear the unmistakable boom of the aunts' voices. All three of them by the sound of it, come to wallow like huge hippos in their little sister's death. The aunts I hated because they look so much like me. You know how it is when you go back to your family. Whatever you've done, whatever you are, you slip back into feeling as if you were a child. Listening to those voices, I lost my grip on Finch and Kelp. They dissolved away like ice-cubes on a bonfire. I was just Janis Mary Finch, another big Simpson girl, whose mother was dead.

'Your manager phoned,' Himmler said from behind me. His voice was still dull, but now it managed to be disapproving as well. 'Said it was urgent. I told her you'd phone her back.'

'No,' I said. 'Not until after the funeral.' Oh, I knew something very, very big must have happened. Mae never fussed about little things. But what did she have to do with Jan Finch? I pushed open the lounge door and stepped into the room.

Immediately I was speared by eight pairs of eyes. Three aunts, one uncle and four cousins. Clever things, eyes. The voices were doing the polite greetings and the mouths were smiling (sadly, of course) but the eyes got the real message across. *Don't think you can ever make it up to Barbara now.*

'Hallo, everyone,' I said.

Auntie Susan sniffed. 'Well, you've changed, I must say.'

'It's only a different haircut.' I ran my fingers through it, thinking, *Mum would have known I'm the same underneath. She wouldn't have been taken in by a haircut and a different set of clothes.*

'Hear you've made a record,' Uncle Nigel said.

'Yes.'

'Doing well, is it?'

'I think it's quite—'

—But you don't need me to spell it out for you, do you? *You* must have stuttered and shuffled and yawned inside when you were trapped into conversations like that. The Auntie Susans and Uncle Nigels of this world make everything boring, even a funeral. I would have given anything to be able to play Finch, to pull her round me like a disguise and make some wild, furious gesture that would shatter all the politenesses. But I couldn't, because I owed it to Mum to be exactly what I was, so the painful, stilted conversation tottered on.

And then Himmler went out to get his coat, so that he would be ready when the cars arrived. I suppose it was thirty seconds or so before he called. I was just avoiding a question about the band when the shout came from the hall.

'Janis!'

I went out. He was standing by the front door, leaning against the telephone table, and his face was dead white.

'Who are those people?' he said. 'By the gate?'

I ducked my head and peered through the little window

beside the front door. I can smell a newspaperman at a hundred paces now, but even then, when I was a mere innocent, there was no mistaking that little cluster in the street, their faces blotched red and green by the colours of the glass.

'Yes,' Himmler said fiercely, not waiting for me to answer. '*Yes.* The ones with the cameras. Would they be anything to do with you?'

I understood then why Mae had been so anxious to speak to me. My hands started to shake. They don't get the cameras out for you if your record's number Three or Number Two.

'*Why?*' Himmler said.

'I think—it must be to do with our record. I think it must—'

'How *dare* you!'

The attack was so sudden, so unlike him, that it threw me. 'What?'

'I thought—' he was struggling to keep his voice steady. '—I thought you'd come here for your mother's sake. To try and make up for the way you'd treated her. I didn't think even *you* would try to use today to your own advantage.'

'What?' I said again. 'You don't mean you think—but that's crazy!'

'Is it?' Himmler waved a hand towards the window. 'Who told them you'd come here for the funeral? It's indecent. You can't even let your mother die without—'

'You shut up!' I held on to the coat-rack with both hands, to stop myself hitting him. 'Don't go on about Mum and me. What do you know about us? Nothing.'

'I know—'

'*Nothing.* Before you came pushing your way in, we were close. Really close.'

'I know you were.' He had regained control of his voice and all at once it went soft, and his eyes sharpened. 'Of course you were close. That's why it hurt her so much when you changed.'

'I haven't changed.'

'Oh, you've changed all right,' Himmler said. 'That's what broke Barbie up. She was never the same after—'

'It's not true.' But I was whispering now. I couldn't take my eyes off his face. 'She would have understood about the money, I know she would. She loved me and she wanted me back.'

'Oh, she wanted you back,' Himmler said bitterly.

The smile that twisted across his face stopped me answering. It would have stopped a fleet of Sherman tanks. For the first time I understood that he hated and resented me even more than I hated and resented him.

'She'd forgiven you for taking the money,' he hissed, 'and she was trying to find you, to tell you she was ill. Until you stamped on her and spat in her face.'

I stared at him. 'What did I do?'

'That's right.' He nodded as if I'd somehow pleased him. 'You don't even know, do you? You sent her money back without even a proper letter, as if you were paying off a taxi driver. Ignoring the fact that she'd married me and changed her name. Oh, she was ill before she got that letter, but that was when she gave up.'

'I didn't—' But I couldn't carry on protesting. I could see that miserable, scrappy letter too clearly. And its scrawled envelope. *Mrs B. Finch*. Written automatically, without remembering what Himmler had told me at Polo's. And now there was no way I could explain to Mum about the tour and the hustle. But it was such a *silly* little thing. I looked away from Himmler's angry, gloating face. 'I don't believe you. I don't believe she saw it like that.'

'No? Want me to show you something?' Taking his wallet out of his inside pocket, he opened it and slid out a thick wad of paper. Must have been a pain to carry around. Ten ten-pound notes, criss-crossed over and over again with sticky tape. 'That's what she thought of your hundred pounds. She wouldn't even have them back when I'd stuck them together.'

'I couldn't tell which picture sickened me more. My frugal mother, carefully shredding all that money into little pieces, or Himmler, grovelling round to pick up the bits so that he could put them together again. I stared at the patchwork.

'Barb wouldn't let me look for you any more after that. Even though I told her about meeting you in the club. She just kept saying, "She's different, Graham, *different*. She'd never have written me a letter like that before she went to London." And then that record of yours came out—'

When your flesh and blood don't give a damn. . . .

'It's not true. I'm not different. I'm the same as I always was and I loved her—'

'Oh yes?' Triumphantly, Himmler waved the bundle of notes at the front door. 'You couldn't even come here, to her funeral, without bringing along a lot of photographers to take pretty pictures of you pretending to be heart-broken and—'

He was yelling and flapping those miserable notes under my nose and suddenly I couldn't bear any more. Couldn't bear his hatred or Mum's death or the fact that it was too late, everything was too late, and I could never straighten things out now. I hit him, hard, on the right cheek-bone.

He fell sideways, cracking his head on the telephone table with a great thump that brought the aunts peering round the door, shocked speechless.

Himmler struggled to his feet, pulling out his hand-kerchief to try and stop the blood running out of his nose. 'You'd never have *hit* me,' he said in a satisfied voice. 'Not before you went to London.'

Then he went upstairs to change his clothes, leaving me staring at my reflection in the hall mirror. Square head, heavy black greatcoat, clenched fist. Finch's reflection.

Chapter 17

Until that moment, I really believed that Finch was a mask. A role that Christie had invented for me. But now, suddenly, we were inseparable and my mother's funeral became Finch's mother's funeral as well. Afterwards, on the train home, the scenes ran over and over in my head, like snatches of a video, proving it to me.

. . . the crematorium chapel, half full of family and friends, all watching me under their eyelids. They all knew, by then, and they had all seen the newspapermen outside. The whispers ran round the chapel while Himmler, on the seat beside me, stared hard at Mum's small coffin. . . .

. . .The little pile of family wreaths in the cloister behind the chapel, with the aunts bending down to read the labels. *I'll take care of that.* Mae had said, and there was a big circle of lilies, showy but severe, with a card tucked into it:

To the best Mum in the world,
Love,
Janis

The aunts didn't say a word, but the angle of their bent backs somehow told me that the whole thing was too expensive, too ostentatious. . . .

. . . The photographers jostling to get a recognizable shot of me walking away from the chapel, while the aunts looked accusing and Himmler made a big thing of not speaking to me. . . .

The photographers.

Slowly, from Coventry to Rugby and Rugby to Milton Keynes, I began to be angry. Not with Himmler. From the moment my fist met his face, I'd done with being angry with Himmler. That was child's play. Now I was angry with the person—whoever it was—who had told the newspapers about Mum's funeral. My mind ran round and round, trying to work out where to put the blame.

Mae?—I suppose it might have struck her as a good sales pitch. But, remembering the gentleness of her voice on the phone, calling me Janis, I found it hard to believe.

Rollo?—Surely not. He—well, I don't have to spell it out, do I? Rollo would shove his head under a steam-hammer if he thought he'd upset me.

Dave?—Dave was into publicity all right, but it was strictly publicity for Dave Lasky. *His* face on the record sleeve. *His* solos getting the applause. It was hard to imagine him deliberately pushing someone else into the limelight.

Job then?—*No frontiers, Finch*, he'd said. Yes, I really think he would have sent the reporters. If he thought it was necessary. But he was the cleverest of us all. He must have seen that there was no point in putting a strain on me—a strain on the whole band—just for the sake of a couple of extra newspaper photographs. Proving the Rat wrong and leaping thirty-seven places up the charts were quite sensational enough.

Or Christie?

Oh God, please God, please don't let it have been Christie. Not now. Not after Bournemouth.

I should have asked, shouldn't I? Leapt out of the train with the question on my lips and not allowed anyone to say anything else until it was answered. And I swear that's exactly what I meant to do. Until we reached Euston.

But, as the train slid along the platform, I saw the others waiting for me. Dave was leaning against a bench, watching out of the corner of his eye in case anyone recognized him, Rollo was staring into the windows of the train, trying to spot me, and Job and Christie were talking together, shoulders hunched, hands in their pockets. A year ago, I'd never heard of them and now they were the nearest thing to a family I'd got.

And one of them had sent the reporters after me to Mum's funeral.

How much family can you afford to lose in a single day? I still wanted my questions answered, but not just at that moment. I couldn't take it. So I stepped off the train without a word and let them crowd round me.

The first few seconds were awkward, because none of them knew how I would be feeling. They watched, they hunted for the proper sort of words—and then Rollo burst in in his usual way.

'You O.K. Finch?'

'Course I'm O.K.' The Finch voice came out automatically, brisk and tough. 'What's the reception committee for? Think I couldn't find my way home?'

'Home?' Dave snorted. 'You won't see much of that for the next couple of days. It's intensive rehearsals until Thursday.'

'Thursday?'

'*Top of the Pops,* you moron.' Rollo had been trying to keep up the sympathy, but when he's excited he has to *move*—dance or drum or turn cart-wheels. Now, beaming at me, he latched on to a stray trolley (which was covered with rat stickers) and raced off down the platform with it, weaving in and out to dodge the people getting off the train.

'Amazing the things that please some people, isn't it?' Dave said.

Job grinned and dug him in the ribs. 'Come on, sunshine, no good trying to kid us. We all know you're dying to get your beautiful face on to a television screen. Even if it is *only* on *Top of the Pops.*'

'But—Thursday?' I said, getting there slowly. 'You mean it's going to be a live programme?'

'Oh, *worse* than that.' Job grinned at me. 'It's not just the programme that's going to be live. We're performing live.'

'*What?*'

'I insisted,' Christie said from behind me. 'Of course I did. 'Face It's not the sort of thing you can mime to.'

All the time the others had been jabbering on at me, I'd been aware of him by my left shoulder, just out of sight. It was like standing with your back to a cliff. You can't see, but you can *feel* the size of the drop behind you, the drop that with one careless step will plunge you deep into dark salt water. Now, as he spoke, his hand closed over my wrist and he stepped round into my field of vision.

'What's the matter with that?' he said. 'Afraid you can't cope?'

'Of course I can cope,' I said briskly. Automatically. And I looked him straight in the eye for the first time since we got back from Bournemouth.

I suppose I was expecting some kind of difference. Not crazy of me, was it? We'd been alone together for four days—four days that were quite unlike anything else in the rest of my life—and I thought there would be something left over, some kind of link between us that hadn't been there before.

But Christie's eyes were the same as they'd always been. Taunting me. Keeping me at a distance. And his brisk voice was like a slap round the face.

'We've got a rehearsal studio booked ready. And a photo-call at half-past five.'

'Give us a chance.' I could match his speaking voice for briskness, but I wasn't sure I could cope with singing yet. 'I've only been off the train for two minutes.'

Christie looked at his watch. 'O.K. We'll drop you off at my mother's and someone can come and fetch you—in an hour?'

No nonsense. How many minutes do you need to put yourself together again, Finch? I wondered how his face would look if I said, *Six months*.

'O.K.' I said.

I let myself into Ida's and, as I went upstairs, I could see the light in the back bedroom. I pushed the door open. She wasn't dusting or anything. Just sitting still on the chair by the controls, staring at the North Star and stroking its funnel very gently with the tip of one finger.

'Hallo, dear,' she said. 'How are you feeling?'

Dead. Empty. Sick of myself.

'O.K.' I said.

Ida nodded. 'Not much point in going on about it, is there? People are very good for the first day or two, but then they get tired of it. Once you've had the funeral, they think that's that. They don't remember that a dead person goes on being dead. On and on and on.' She wasn't moaning. Just stating facts, while her finger went on stroking the North Star. 'I still miss him, you know.'

I stood there, like the Statue of Liberty, huge and dumb. What she was saying wasn't exactly comforting, but at least it was part of the world I was in at the moment—unlike all that chat about *Top of the Pops.*

'You'd be better for a lie down and a drink.' Ida slid out under the rails, taking my hand as she stood up.

I nodded. 'I wouldn't mind some cocoa.'

'*And* a lie down,' she said firmly. 'All funerals are bad enough, but that one must have been worse than most. With the reporters on top of everything.'

It took a moment. She was half-way through the door before I really heard what she'd said. Then my arms shot out and I grabbed her shoulders.

'*What?*' I turned her round to face me. 'What do you know about reporters? Who told them where I was?'

Her eyes shifted. Went blank and slipped away from mine. 'Told them?'

'Ida!' I shook her. 'Someone set the reporters on to me. When I find out who did it, I'll mash them. *Who phoned the newspapers?*'

Flick, flick. Her eyes went nervously from one side of the room to the other, working things out. '*I* did,' she said. 'At least, I didn't, but I was the one who told the papers. Someone phoned up asking for you, and I was flummoxed, so I told them where you were.'

Then I knew. For sure. 'That's right,' I said gently. 'And

then you telephoned all the other papers didn't you? Just to make things fair.'

'I—' she went pink and her voice stumbled.

'Come off it, Ida.' I let go of her, very carefully and straightened her cardigan, concentrating on the pattern of the stitches and the shape of the buttons. Trying to shake off the picture of Christie taking the receiver out of her hand while she dithered. *O.K., Mum. I'll handle this.* And then, afterwards, dialling and dialling and dialling. 'What did he think he was up to?'

'He said—' She gulped and then spoke more slowly, as if she was puzzled. 'He said, "She's stopped fighting. She's shrivelling up. She's got to have some kind of shock to get her angry and get her going again." I can remember it exactly, but I don't know what he meant.'

I looked down at my hands. 'I know what he meant.' But I didn't spell it out for her. I was almost too angry to speak at all.

'I'm sorry,' Ida said. 'What can I do? Do you still want the cocoa?'

'No. Thank you.' None of my anger was for her. It was very cold, very controlled and all for Christie. 'I want to think.'

'But you ought to have something—'

'I'll tell you what I want,' I said. It came to me quite suddenly, out of the blue. 'I want to run the engine.'

'But you can't! Christie'll—' She bit the words off short and dropped her eyes. 'All right. I'll show you how.'

For maybe five minutes she watched me, terrified that I was going to run berserk and start ripping up the rails or pulling wires out of the controls. But it finally got through to her that I was safe and she slid out, shutting the door behind her.

I went on running the North Star, watching the wheels roll on and on, completely under my control, pulling the carriages I coupled up to it and going where I set the points for it to go. With no will of its own. As it ran, I thought about the band. Not about Christie so much, but about Rollo and Job and Dave, who would all suffer if I simply walked out and refused to sing with Christie any more.

I couldn't do it to them. I couldn't be the one who smashed things up.

But I couldn't go on moving to Christie's orders any more, either. Being the person he had made me and doing and feeling what he wanted.

Round and round went the North Star and round and round after it went my thoughts, while the bearded face of Isambard Kingdom Brunel looked down at me from the wall, out of its setting of enormous chains. Round and round and round.

Ten minutes before Dave came to pick me up, I switched off the controls and ducked out of the room, closing the door carefully after me. I knew exactly what I was going to do to get my own back on Christie.

Chapter 18

But first there were the next two days to get through. Somehow I had to stay calm and not give my feelings away to Christie and the only way to do that was to avoid him. While we were rehearsing, I could just about manage to concentrate on the song and forget that I wanted to lash out at him and batter his face, but the moment we finished rehearsing I had to think of an excuse to leave. I had my hair cut—even though it didn't really need it—I went home to mend a mythical tear in my *ninja* suit and I made twice the normal number of trips to the bog.

By the end of Wednesday, I was beginning to think I'd never survive. We had spent nearly all the day together, rehearsing and doing interviews and having discussions with Zombie, and everywhere I turned, Christie's face seemed to have been watching me. When we came out of the Zombie offices, he looked at his watch.

'Time to eat. Let's go back to the flat and get something from Mr Liu. Then we can just run over tomorrow's details again.'

'*Again?*' Dave sighed loudly and rolled his eyes up towards the sky.

'Well, we ought to be quite sure—'

'I *am* quite sure,' I said. 'Don't know about the rest of you, but what I need is a break. You made me miss my karate lesson today, Christie, and I'm going to go insane if I don't get some exercise. Drop me off at your mum's and I'll go round to see Bernard.'

None of them liked it very much. Somehow they were all feeling that we should stick together, as if we'd been hit by an earthquake instead of a Number One single. But I ignored the surprised looks and the odd comments and jumped thankfully out of the van at Ida's.

When I got round to the dojo, there was a class in progress and Bernard was busy with a dozen little boys. Bowing in his direction, I took myself off to the punch-bags at the end of the room. I hadn't come expecting a lesson. What I needed was a place to practise what I already knew. I warmed up briefly and then took out the nunchaku that Christie had given me.

It's a very personal weapon and there's room for working out your own way of using it, but basically its effectiveness is a matter of timing. Unscrewing it, I gripped one end, settling my fingers into a comfortable grip, and began to whirl it through the air, getting back the feel of the other half of the stick moving on the end of the chain. When I was happy with it, I started to attack the hardest punch-bag, concentrating on accurate aim and maximum impact.

I was concentrating so hard that I didn't really notice when the little boys collected their things and filed out. What interrupted me was Bernard's voice.

'Who is it?'

I let my arm drop. 'Who what?'

'I can always tell when someone stops practising a martial art for its own sake and begins to think of attacking an enemy. A look in the eyes, perhaps, and an extra bite to the blows. You've got the look of a person who wants to kill someone Finch.'

'Not kill,' I said quickly.

He watched me before he spoke again. 'Christie?'

It's not easy to lie to your karate teacher. In a strange way, you're very close and you sense things about each other. Now, as I hesitated for a second, he nodded.

'I thought that was it. It's in your voice on the record. However much you scream at him, there's—oh, I don't know. A link. I don't know if it's love or hate, but it's very strong.'

'Oh yes, yes.' I lashed out at the punch-bag again, but

like an angry child this time. 'Go on, tell me I've made a fool of myself.'

'Not a fool. Nothing foolish about having feelings, is there?'

'Not if you keep them to yourself,' I said fiercely. 'But it's pretty dumb to be tricked into spilling them out on vinyl for the whole world to laugh at, isn't it?'

Bernard shook his head. 'Who's laughing, Finch? It's that feeling, between you and Christie, that made your record take off. It's unforgettable. And I imagine that it's what made the Rat uncomfortable about it, as well. I should think he's a very cold person and he couldn't take the strength of it.'

'That makes two of us.' I began to coil the chain so that I could screw the nunchaku together again. '*I* didn't choose to show myself up like that. I knew I was singing about my real life, but I thought it was my past life. Christie *tricked* me.'

'But that's how he works, isn't it?' Bernard shrugged. 'He takes far more than he gives and uses even the feelings you have for him. He's very insecure.'

Now it was my turn to say, 'Christie?' Disbelievingly.

Bernard's not given to spelling things out. He'll show you once and then you're on your own. So he didn't answer my question, but just shrugged and began to talk, instead, about improving my aim with the nunchaku.

But if he thought he had altered what I was thinking, he was way, way off beam. I seemed to be past thinking. My mind was fixed, very steadily, on what I was going to do to Christie on Thursday and there was no room for anyone to change it. Christie had made me into Finch and Finch was about to have her revenge.

I needed to make very careful, detailed plans, because I had so little privacy. Anyone else in the band was quite likely to open the suitcase I took to the *Top of the Pops* studio and trying to smuggle anything in with me that was liable to ruin my chances and make the whole thing blow up in my face. So I waited. I waited until the very last instant, when we were all in the van outside Ida's and Job had just turned on the ignition. Then I yelped.

'My *tabi* boots!'

'No one's going to look at your *feet,*' Dave said.

'So I appear on television in these?' I tapped the red wellingtons I'd borrowed from Ida. 'Don't be thick. It'll only take a minute to get them, and I need something a bit warmer to wear, as well.'

Leaping out of the van, I let myself into the house and streaked upstairs. I had the bundle all ready on my bed, the boots and everything else wrapped up in an enormous black jumper. Holding it firmly in both arms, I started down again.

'Oh, it *is* you.' Ida popped her head out of the lounge. 'I thought you'd gone.'

'I have really. Just forgot these.'

'Well, I'm glad I saw you. I wanted to have a chance to wish you luck.' She took a step towards me. 'You've been very good to me, Janis dear, and I don't want you to think I don't appreciate it.'

Typical Ida. Choosing the moment when you're just off to the biggest event of your life to make an emotional scene. I managed an awkward grin.

'It's been O.K. I mean—it's good of you to have me here.'

'Oh, you're like a daughter in the house.'

I saw her hand coming towards me, ready to grip mine, and I side-stepped quickly to avoid it. A mistake. Instead of closing on my hand, her fingers closed on the top of my jumper, round the lumps underneath. I saw her eyes change as she felt, and understood, what I had there.

'Ida—' I said. But she interrupted me.

'You're like a *daughter,*' she said again. 'Christie was always more fond of his dad.' She paused '*Very* fond of his dad, he was. In fact, I don't think he's ever quite got over George's death. He doesn't seem to get close to many people.'

Then, quite deliberately, she patted the jumper and

moved back, letting me past to the door. Letting me go with what I had in my arms. I smiled, rather taken aback, but before I could say anything else Job hooted from outside and I was on my way.

A television studio's not an easy place for secret plans. From the moment you walk in, they want to tie you down, to practise camera angles and lighting and get you made up and predictable. If you think what *Top of the Pops* is like, with all those stages, and the lights, and the smoke and the audience dancing about, you'll see how carefully it has to be organized to stop things going wrong. And they were being especially careful with us, because we'd come from nowhere, not knowing the ropes, and we were the people that everyone would be waiting to see.

But I'd worked all that into my plan. From the very first run through, I went on with the black bag I always took on stage with me. In its time, it had held posters that I tore up, glass that I smashed, water pistols that I used to end the set with a steady fountain of water falling on to my face. That day, it was full of empty beer cans. Everyone grinned as I lined them up and when I stamped them flat, as the song reached its climax, the cheer-leaders began to improvise a stamping dance. Great. Everyone loved it. Oh sure, it hurt to stamp on the cans in soft *tabi* boots, but I knew how to time things and anyway, what's a bit of suffering when you're planning a revenge?

All the time I was perfectly calm. I joked around with Rollo and Dave and discussed what was going on with Job. The only person I avoided—the only person I couldn't bear to speak to—was Christie. I could see him watching me and I knew he was wondering what was going to happen, but that didn't worry me. He would never guess. Never in a million years.

The hardest part was getting away from them all, after the final run through, so that I could change what was in my bag. Rollo stuck to me like superglue. Poor Rollo. I knew what he was thinking. He was probably the only person apart from me who still remembered about Mum's funeral and thought that I might be affected by it. But, however gently, I had to give him the chop or he'd spoil everything. I muttered something about needing a bit of space to psyche up for the perfomance and he backed off at top speed, muttering apologies and leaving me alone in the dressing-room.

Flattening the last of the beer cans, I threw them into the bin and then lifted my big black jumper out of the corner where I'd stashed it. Very carefully, holding my breath in case something had gone wrong, I unrolled it.

The North Star looked bright and beautiful and totally irreplaceable. For a second I stared down at it and then I picked it up and slipped it into my bag. Down the side of the bag, I slid the other thing that was wrapped in the jumper. That disguised the shape of the engine a bit—and anyway, beer cans are pretty lumpy. I was fairly sure that no one would notice. Hoisting the bag on to my shoulder, I marched out of the dressing-room and went to find the others.

Don't expect me to tell you about the show. Oh, I know all about how it works now. Should do, after all the times we've been on it. But that day I couldn't take in anything at all. I was too nervous and too busy keeping my bag beside me and out of harm's way. I felt as though electric shocks were going through my stomach and, all the time, I could see Christie watching me.

Then we were on. Massive cheers, lights in our eyes and the music coming out automatically.

'Came out of Birmingham with nothing. . . .'

After the first couple of lines, I got a grip on it and I could start getting myself ready. They're not big, those *Top of the Pops* stages, but Christie and I were on opposite sides and it would take him a couple of strides to reach me. Space enough, if I got everything right.

I waited until he began on the rap in that low, spiky voice.

'Come on and face the fact you'll be walking in mist. . . .'

Then, still singing, still keeping my melody riding over the top, I swung the bag off my shoulder, exactly as we'd rehearsed, and opened the top.

I had to admire Christie's reaction when I took out the North Star. 'Face It' is a very intricate song to sing, especially when the instruments and the melody and the rap are all working together. Get one of them even slightly wrong and the whole thing turns into a hopeless jumble. Christie didn't let his voice waver, not for a second. But I could see from his eyes that he'd got the message. If he tried to come and take the engine away from me, twelve million people would see Finch and Christie Joyce squabbling over a toy train. And that would be the end of our image, of the eerie link between us and the idea of Kelp as a serious band. No amount of explanations afterwards would ever wipe out that childish picture.

His mind went exactly the way I'd predicted to myself. Glancing down, he checked that I was still wearing the *tabi* boots. I was. And there wasn't a chance that I could do much real damage to the North Star with those. *Just a threat. No need to take her seriously.* Oh, it almost made me shudder to read his thoughts so easily.

I gave him a minute's grace, to lull him into a false sense of security. Then, when he was well into the second half of the rap—

'There's no disguise that'll hide your eyes. . . .'

—I slipped my hand into the bag again. And yes, it was all part of the plan. I had chosen the timing exactly, to turn the song back on him, so that he would understand that he was going to be made to give himself away in public. In just the way he had given me away.

I took out the nunchaku.

He understood, all right. I think he understood even before he saw what I was getting out. His eyes widened and his fists clenched, and they went on widening and clenching as I unscrewed the nunchaku and stretched the length of chain against my cheek.

Then we were into the last section of the song, the section when the voices taunt me in pairs—Rollo and Dave, Job and Christie—while I sing fierce, hard notes without any words over the top. That's when I'd stamped the beer cans in rehearsals, adding their crunch to the noise of the percussion. Now, as my voice rose, I began to whirl the nunchaku over my head, round and round, gathering speed.

Right, Christie Joyce, this is it! Your band or your engine? I'm in charge now, and I'm giving you the choice. You've bullied me and used me and built your band's success on my private feelings and now you're going to have to give as much as I've given.

Ever wondered how Frankenstein felt when his monster went out of control? I hoped that Christie was going through all that and more. Whirling the nunchaku faster and faster, I kept my eyes fixed on the engine, building up to a crashing destructive blow at the loudest moment of the song.

But, just before I took my final aim, I glanced up, towards Christie. I suppose I wanted to taste my triumph. I was pretty sure that he would choose to lose the engine and save the band, and I wanted to see his helpless anger.

He was crying.

He was standing quite still, as always, with the song coming steadily out of his mouth, every note perfect, and tears were running down his face.

I felt as though I had never seen him before. Oh sure, my mind had been full of Christie for months, but that was a huge, strong, dark Christie who loomed over me like a giant in a fairy-tale, cutting out the light.

A Christie I'd made for myself, the way he made Finch?

I didn't know. All I knew was that what I was watching now was real, so real that, like an answer, the tears started running down my face as well. *I'm sorry*. I wanted to say. *I never looked at you properly before, Christie, but I'm looking now*. I had to make him understand, but the song was all around us and it seemed impossible to escape from the pattern it forced us into.

Then, as I opened my mouth to sing the last slow line, the right movements came to me. Taking the two steps across the stage that brought me to Christie, I held out the nunchaku to him. He took one end of it and that's how we were as the end of the melody floated out over the studio. Side by side, joined by the short, strong chain.

Came out of Birmingham with nothing
Junked the name and face I used to wear
When your flesh and blood don't give a damn
Your luggage doesn't hold much from before

My last coins went to pay for coffee—
Come on and face the fact you'll be walking in mist
and the earth'll move—sure, but under your feet
Strange reflections by the motorway—
If you're set on leaving, we won't deceive you
and a stake in our future means you'll have to wait
Then the place exploded with the band
Don't go dreaming of love or fame
And there was music in the sad café
Because sorry, girl, but we've only got music
and that won't hold you or keep you warm.

Put your body where your mind is
Let them rise together
But remember it's the music
But remember it's only the music

Before the evening hit disaster
You can't duck the fact that it's a switch-blade playground
and the knives are out for the face in front
First I heard the music of the band
There's no disguise that'll hide your eyes
if you put yourself up where the fingers point
Found there was a voice to match my voice
Don't fool yourself that no one'll know
Discovered I could lose myself in sound
Because if you're not sure and you don't stand solid
then the pressure will crack you and the cracks will show.

Put your body where your mind is
Let them rise together
But remember it's the music
But remember it's only the music

Come on and face the fact that you're out on your own

Put your body where your mind is
Let them rise together
But remember it's the music

Face it!
But remember it's only the music
Face it!
It's only the music
Face it!
Face it!
The music . . .

. . . I came out of Birmingham with nothing. . . .

Other Books by Gillian Cross

Tightrope

ISBN 0 19 271750 2 (paperback)
ISBN 0 19 271804 5 (hardback)

Eddie Beale looks after his friends, people say, as long as they entertain him. When he takes notice of Ashley, she is happy to put on a show and be part of the excitement that surrounds him and his gang—it is a relief from the unrelenting drudgery of her life. Then she realizes that someone is watching her. Someone is stalking her and leaving messages that get uglier and uglier. Can Eddie help her? And if he does, what price will she have to pay?

The Great Elephant Chase

ISBN 0 19 271786 3
Winner of The Smarties Prize and the
Whitbread Children's Novel Award

The elephant changed their lives for ever. Because of the elephant, Tad and Cissie become entangled in a chase across America, by train, by flatboat and steam boat. Close behind is Hannibal Jackson, who is determined to have the elephant for himself. And how do you hide an enormous Indian elephant?

Wolf

ISBN 0 19 271784 7
Winner of the Carnegie Medal

Cassy hears sinister footsteps in the middle of the night. Suddenly she is packed off to stay with her beautiful, feckless mother. There is no explanation. Something has gone frighteningly wrong.

Danger is coming after Cassy. And behind it lurks the dark wolf-shape that seems to slink into everything.

Even her dreams.

Pictures in the Dark

ISBN 0 19 271741 3

When Charlie takes the photograph of the unknown animal swimming in the river that night, he has no idea of the effect it will have on his life and the weird events it will set in motion.

Why is Peter, the boy with the strange, staring eyes, so obsessed by the picture? And what is it about Peter that upsets everybody so much—even his own father?

When Charlie tries to help Peter and protect him from the bullying, he is led deeper into the secret, mysterious life of the river bank, and the creatures that inhabit it.

New World

ISBN 0 19 271723 5

'I'm helping to test a game—and it's brilliant. I'm even getting paid for doing it . . .'

But are things really that simple?

When Miriam and Stuart step into the shifting, addictive world of virtual reality, every move they make is monitored. Hesketh, who developed the game, is determined that the tests will succeed. So is the games company which has millions invested in the New World project. Miriam and Stuart are the guinea-pigs and, as the game tightens its hold, they become aware that something—or someone—is playing on their deepest, secret fears. Is this part of the tests? Or has someone broken into the game?

The Iron Way

ISBN 0 19 271639 5

For Jem and Kate, nothing will ever be the same again. Conor changes their lives—just as the railway he is helping to build will change the country. Jem and Kate see a chance of escaping from their miserable poverty and finding happiness. But not everyone welcomes change. Although the railway brings excitement and opportunity, it brings conflict too.

The past and the future meet head-on, and Jem and Kate are caught in the middle. What will happen when the violence explodes?

The Demon Headmaster Series

The Demon Headmaster
ISBN 0 19 271742 1

On the first day at her new school, Dinah realizes that something is horribly wrong. All the children are neat and well-behaved and the prefects are like secret police. Dinah is determined to get to the bottom of it. But what will happen when she looks into the terrible green eyes of the Demon Headmaster?

The Prime Minister's Brain
ISBN 0 19 271743 X

Dinah and her friends discover that the Demon Headmaster is planning to hypnotize the Prime Minister and control the country! Can they foil the plot?

The Revenge of the Demon Headmaster
ISBN 0 19 271744 8

Suddenly everyone's mad about Hunky Parker. People are desperate to buy disgusting Hunky T-shirts, trainers like pigs' trotters, and pig-swill yoghurt. And they long for a holiday in The Sty where there is sun and swimming one day and skiing the next.

But Dinah hates it all. And when she and her friends try to investigate, they walk straight into the middle of a fiendish plot—and a race against time. Can they find out what is going on? Can they stop the Demon Headmaster before it's too late?

The Demon Headmaster Strikes Again
ISBN 0 19 271453 8

When the Hunter family are persuaded to move house, Dinah, Lloyd, and Harvey realize that there is something very strange about the new village. And soon Dinah suspects that their old enemy, the Demon Headmaster, is back. This time, he has got control of a research laboratory, and he's planning to take over Nature itself. But to do that, he needs Dinah. And that means she's in terrible danger . . .

The Demon Headmaster Takes Over

ISBN 0 19 271758 8

Suddenly, asking questions is dangerous—and finding out the answers seems impossible.

What's going on? Dinah and SPLAT investigate, and their search leads them to the Hyperbrain—a computer with more-than-human intelligence.

Who is the mysterious Controller in charge of the Hyperbrain? He sounds horribly like the Demon Headmaster, but the Headmaster has vanished for ever . . . Or has he?

Other Oxford Fiction

It's My Life
Michael Harrison
ISBN 0 19 275042 9

As soon as he opens his front door, Martin feels that something's wrong. But he never expects the hand over his mouth, the rope around his wrists, and the mysterious man who's after a large ransom. Before Martin knows it, he's a pawn in a dangerous game that becomes more and more terrifying with every turn . . .

A Haunted Year
Ann Phillips
ISBN 0 19 275046 1

Florence is bored. The Easter holidays are dragging on—until she finds a way to summon up a ghost.

Now she has a friend to play with. George always comes when she calls him. And soon she doesn't even need to call him. And then—he won't go away . . .

No matter what Florence does or where she goes, George is always there!

Against the Day
Michael Cronin
ISBN 0 19 275039 9

It is 1940. The Nazis have invaded, and Britain is now part of the Third Reich. All over the country, German military authorities are taking control, led by the brutal Gestapo.

But slowly, surely, a resistance is building throughout the land. A secret network of people are plotting to overthrow the Nazis and win back their freedom, at any cost. Frank and Les, two schoolboys, never meant to get involved—but find themselves part of a dangerous undercover operation that can only end in bloodshed . . .

Humanzee
Susan Gates
ISBN 0 19 275038 0

Nemo has seen some amazing sights in his circus life, but nothing matches Chingwe the humanzee in the Wonderland freak show. One look at the creature—part human, part chimpanzee—sends Nemo into a rage. You can't put people in cages!

Nemo rescues Chingwe and takes him home but quickly learns that not everyone shares his tolerance. The men with guns, for instance, who want to see Chingwe destroyed . . .

A Pack of Lies
Geraldine McCaughrean
ISBN 0 19 275016 X
Winner of the Carnegie Medal and the Guardian Children's Fiction Award

Ailsa Povey doesn't trust MCC Berkshire, the mysterious man helping out in her mother's antique shop. He dazzles every customer with enchanting stories about the antiques, but Ailsa knows it's all a big pack of lies.

Yet still the stories come thick and fast: tales of adventure, revenge, mystery, and horror. Now only one story remains to be told—that of MCC himself. Who is he? Where is he from? And, most importantly, what does he want from the Poveys?

Chandra
Frances Mary Hendry
ISBN 0 19 275058 5
Winner of the Writer's Guild Award and the Lancashire Book Award

Chandra can't believe her luck. The boy her parents have chosen for her to marry seems to be modern and open-minded. She's sure they will have a wonderful life together. So once they are married she travels out to the desert to live with him and his family—only when she gets there, things are not as she imagined.

Alone in her darkened room she tries to keep her strength and her identity. She is Chandra and she won't let it be forgotten.

Facing the Dark
Michael Harrison
ISBN 0 19 271801 0

The son of a murderer—that's what they called Simon. His father is in jail, accused of the murder of a rival cab driver. Then Simon meets Charley, grieving for her dead father, the murdered man.

Against the odds Simon and Charley become friends. Together they determine to find out the real story behind the murder. Together they face the danger that surrounds them and bring back some hope for the future.

Sea Dance
Will Gatti
ISBN 0 19 271803 7

Willie Cormack hates the sea. He sees it in his nightmares, the savage ocean full of the ghosts of drowned fishermen, hands reaching out to pull him down into the dark.

Then the tiny community in which he lives is thrown into turmoil by a lone sailor who is suddenly thrust among them. In the atmosphere of bigotry and suspicion that follows, a terrible tragedy seems inevitable unless Willie can overcome his fears. Can he pit himself against the elements that haunt his dreams? Can he face the raging sea?

Nowhere to Run
Sue Welford
ISBN 0 19 271808 5

A few drunken moments at a party and Cass's world is turned upside-down. She has broken all her own resolutions and betrayed her parents' trust. Now she has an agonizing decision to make which will affect all their lives. Amid all the turmoil and heartbreak, there is only one person who seems to understand what Cass is going through—the last person in the world that Cass would have chosen as a friend, the yobbish bully, James Derwent.

But James has problems of his own, and when these reach a crisis can Cass help him as he had helped her? And will she be in time . . .

River Boy
Tim Bowler
ISBN 0 19 275035 6
Winner of the Carnegie Medal

Standing at the top of the fall, framed against the sky, was the figure of a boy. At least, it looked like a boy, though he was quite tall and it was hard to make out his features against the glare of the sun. She watched and waited, uncertain what to do, and whether she had been seen.

When Jess's grandfather has a serious heart attack, surely their planned trip to his boyhood home will have to be cancelled? But Grandpa insists on going so that he can finish his final painting, 'River Boy'. As Jess helps her ailing grandfather with his work, she becomes entranced by the scene he is painting. And then she becomes aware of a strange presence in the river, the figure of a boy, asking her for help and issuing a challenge that will stretch her swimming talents to the limits. But can she take up the challenge before it is too late for Grandpa . . . and the River Boy?

'a superbly written, well-crafted story.'
School Librarian

'*River Boy* has all the hallmarks of a classic . . . You are not the same person at the end of this book.'
Carnegie Medal Judges

'an accomplished, crafted book.'
Times Educational Supplement

'haunting, poetic and written with great feeling.'
Mail on Sunday

'strong on mood and atmosphere.'
The Guardian

'The atmosphere is haunting . . .'
The Spectator

'Bowler's writing creates indelible visual images.'
Time Out

Also by Tim Bowler

Shadows

ISBN 0 19 271802 9

Jamie's father keeps driving him on to win, to become a world squash champion. But Jamie can't take it any more. He decides to run away with the girl he finds hiding in the shadows, trying to escape from the danger that pursues her.

After a while Jamie realizes he can't run away for ever. He has to come out of the shadows and face up to his father, whatever the cost.

Dragon's Rock

ISBN 0 19 275036 4

Benjamin knows he shouldn't have taken the stone from Dragon's Rock. Ever since then, he's had the same terrifying nightmare of the dragon that chases him, breath like a furnace, roaring in fury, racing faster, faster . . .

Midget

ISBN 0 19 275037 2

Midget doesn't have much going for him. He's fifteen years old, three foot tall, and puny as anything. He's trapped in a useless, twitching body he can't control, tortured by Seb, his cruel older brother, and can only communicate in grunts and gestures.

But Midget knows one thing—sailing. He dreams of sailing his own boat, and showing Seb a thing or two. Everyone says it'll take a miracle, but that's when Midget starts to realize that even miracles are possible. It's just that sometimes they hurt people who get in the way . . .

'a masterly handling of suspense and cold trickling horror'

Sunday Telegraph